Then Came Christmas

A Tom Doherty Associates Book

New York

Then Came Christmas

Randy Lee Eickhoff

THEN CAME CHRISTMAS

Copyright © 2002 by Randy Lee Eickhoff

This book is printed on acid-free paper.

Book design by Jane Adele Regina

Excerpt from "Journey of the Magi" in *Collected Poems 1909–1962* by T. S. Eliot, copyright 1936 by Harcourt, Inc., copyright © 1964, 1963 by T. S. Eliot, reprinted by permission of the publisher.

A Forge Book
Published by Tom Doherty Associates, LLC
175 Fifth Avenue
New York, NY 10010

www.tor.com

Forge® is a registered trademark of Tom Doherty Associates, LLC.

ISBN 0-765-30142-3

First Edition: October 2002

Printed in the United States of America

0 9 8 7 6 5 4 3 2 1

In memory of
RAYMOND J. EICKHOFF,
who loved Christmas so much

And for Robert Cloud,

without whom

this could not have been written

And Cain talked with Abel his brother: and it came to pass, when they were in the field, that Cain rose up against Abel his brother, and slew him.

And the Lord said unto Cain, Where is Abel thy brother? And he said, I know not: Am I my brother's keeper?

Genesis 4:8–9

And when they were come into the house, they saw the young child with Mary his mother, and fell down, and worshipped him: and when they had opened their treasures, they presented unto him gifts; gold, and frankincense, and myrrh.

Matthew 2:11

"A cold coming we had of it,
Just the worst time of the year. . . ."

T. S. Eliot,
"Journey of the Magi"

Then Came Christmas

Chapter I

That year my birthday fell on Thanksgiving as it did every few years, and so I knew the year was going to be something special. Pa always said that happened due to the turning of the earth, but in my youthful mind I reckoned it to be something wonderful and magical. I always seemed to get the best presents on those years, and I remember those years as golden. Fall—we called it Indian summer—seemed to hang around a bit longer than usual, and the days had this rich, deep look to them as if they were tinged with a soft golden light, and the air had a smoky taste to it like a pile of old leaves before you put a match to them. The cottonwoods held onto their yellow leaves, and the oaks and maples their russets and browns well into November, before reluctantly releasing them just before the first snow, around Pearl Harbor Day.

That first snow always seemed to be a gentle one, with huge fluffy flakes falling faintly from the night sky just before Mom shoved me protesting up the stairs to my room beneath the eaves at bedtime. I knew that in the morning the pastures and the hill leading down to the stock dam below the house would be deep with snow. Pa would have already been down to the tack room and brought up my Silver Racer sled for me to use after breakfast. He would rub rust from the runners with a handful of steel wool while I gathered the eggs from the henhouse and brought in split kindling to refill the wood bin beside the huge stone fireplace in the living room.

Then the rest of the day would pretty much be mine as long as I didn't saddle up Spotty, my pinto, and ride over to the Sutter place to see Franny or else to the Stone place to visit with Johnny Stone, my best friend. Then I had to take care of Spotty before I did anything else. Pa was a stickler on that. The stock always came first on the Bar X—so called because we were ten miles from Ithaca. I would have to wipe Spotty down and brush him if I took him out before I did anything else. A rider always took care of her horse first and didn't trust that job to anyone else, so she knew the job had been done right, Pa always said. I reckon that was a holdover from the old days when a man's life depended often on his horse and knowing everything he could know about his horse.

Franny was a couple of years older than me, but that didn't seem to matter much to us, because we didn't play with dolls and such. Mostly, we talked about riding and barrel racing and pole bending because those were the only two events for girls in the rodeos. That year, however, she always seemed to have this secret little smile on her lips whenever a boy came up to her to say hello in the schoolyard in Ithaca while she was talking with some of her friends. Her friends, usually Ena May and Tillie Harkins, giggled behind their hands when the boys came up, but I pretended not to notice although that would annoy me some. Those boys would get this strange little smile on their faces, and they always seemed to want to know if one of the girls might want to take a walk out behind the schoolhouse and smell the honeysuckle. One time Jimmie Traylor butted in when I was talking to Franny to ask if she wanted to go check the honeysuckle with him, and I got all fired up mad and said he was a fool because the honeysuckle had finished blooming a month ago, and all the girls held their hands over their mouths and giggled. Jimmie got this silly grin on his face and said I was the fool because the honeysuckle *he* was talking about was always in bloom, and he winked at Franny, who laughed out loud and gave me this look that made me mad. So I hauled off and pasted Jimmie smack on his winking eye. He fell to his knees and howled that I had blinded him some, and the girls did that little tsk-tsking and well-I-never that made them seem like they had watched too many June Allyson movies. Franny let on that I wasn't being ladylike, and before I took full stock of what I was doing, I popped her on her nose and blood spattered everywhere. There was no telling who I might have laid into next, but one of the teachers, Miss Strawheim, had me by the back of my collar and marched me into the schoolhouse and kept me after school dusting erasers. Mom had to come and get me, and Miss Strawheim told her what I had done, and I got another be-a-lady lecture all the way home and into supper. I had to call Franny and tell her how sorry I was for hitting her like that, but Franny just gave me this *humph!* and said something like wasn't it time I grew up? Somewhere around when she got to talking about how *Peter Pan* was only a movie and Jimmie *was* kind of cute and all, the way his cowlick swept across his forehead, I'd had all I could take for the evening and hung up. I saw her the next day at school, standing in a little crowd of girls, but when I walked toward them, Franny leaned over and whispered something in Ena May's ear, and the girls looked at me and burst out laughing. For some reason, the back of my neck grew warm, and I could feel my ears burning as I watched her disgustedly, simpering and flirting with the boys. When I mentioned this to Stocker, Pa's hired hand, he just laughed and mumbled something about trees and sap rising in the boys, which confused me even more because everyone knew sap rose in the spring, and when I mentioned this to him, he just snickered and said he wasn't talking about that kind of rising. I gave up, figuring it was just one of those things adults said I'd understand when I got older.

I never knew quite how to take Stocker. He was a drinker of hard corn whiskey from Old Man Ferris's still over by the Badlands. Stocker claimed that he took only a nip now and then for medicinal purposes. That could be. But I never have known anyone with so many ailments as ol' Stocker—nor a philosopher with such a conviction that the whole world was veering off at an angle contrary to his interests. Pa said Stocker came by his reasoning rightful enough, having been a sawyer for a logging company in the Black Hills near Hill City before he came to work for us. I guess there was something about doing that kind of work that turned a man into a homespun Socrates. Maybe it was the cutting of the trees that did it. I don't know. He always seemed to come up with one saying or another for something that happened, even if they didn't mean much. Like when someone stole Oly Anderson's pickup, and Stocker said the whole world was a straw and everyone sucked. That was Stocker.

On the Saturday before that Thanksgiving, I was eight miles away from the ranch as the crow flies, down at White Shale Creek, which ran from our dam to the Bad River, gathering rose hips for Mom, who always made a tonic against the winter cold from some of them and jellied the rest. Mom was in one of her persnickety moods, snapping at everyone right and left. She had tired circles under her eyes lately, and today her lips pressed together tight as if she had a bellyache. When I slammed into the kitchen for the third time, I found a milk pail shoved into my hand and myself back out the door before I could draw a deep breath. Idle hands are for the devil's mischief, she snapped irritably after I protested, and I knew enough to keep my mouth shut on that. When Mom got to spouting Bible stuff, both Pa and me cut her a wide rein. I frowned as I rode down toward the creosote wood railroad trestle running past the old homestead. Mom had been becoming more and more distant—almost as if she was going into a retreat, away from the commonplace sinners around her. She had become, well, mystical and a bit more fanatical with church. Of course, that could have been simply the season, as we were coming into Halloween and all, but she had also taken to reading Christian Science material. It was almost like she was trying to convince herself that she was going to live forever. But I didn't make those connections, then. I was just confused because I didn't know what to expect from her from one day to the next.

I sighed and made my way through the thick brush above the homestead. Chokecherry branches scraped against the side of the pail and rasped across my jeans. Squirrels hopped along the ground in the plum thicket at the other end of the clearing, and high overhead, a golden eagle hovered motionlessly on a slipstream in the sepia sun, watching carefully in hopes that I would flush a squirrel or field mouse out into the open for him. The cries of the jays and meadowlarks and doves at the river's edge lifted sharp with warning. I always griped and moaned, pretending that I didn't like to go down to the creek and gather the berries and such that Mom brewed her magic elixirs from, but secretly I enjoyed it. I didn't tell Stinky

Porter or Johnny Stone that I liked to do such "girl stuff,"
though, 'cause I had a hard enough time living down being a
girl and such and convincing them that I could still do those
certain things that guys did. Like when you hit your thumb
with a hammer and wanted to cry but just knew you couldn't
'cause you would be teased the rest of your life for being a
sissy.

This day, however, I was alone with the milk pail that
Mom had given me along with instructions not to come back
before I had filled it with rose hips. Spotty nickered and con-
tentedly nudged a few strands of grama grass from where I
had picketed him under the railroad trestle next to the creosote black timbers. I flushed a grouse when I entered the plum
thicket, making my way down to the creek bank where the
wild roses grew, working my way carefully. Wild roses could
be as treacherous as barbed wire.

I took a deep breath, enjoying the feel of the sun on my
shoulders beneath the red-and-yellow-checked Tom Sawyer
flannel shirt I wore against the slight chill. The day seemed
smoky, and I paused at the rusted pump that stood next to
the old gray-boarded house in the center of the clearing to
take another deep breath, enjoying the smell of old, rotting
wood and sour earth, and the slight musty smell of moldy
vegetables that came from the old root cellar dug into the
small hill behind the old clapboard house.

The outhouse had fallen in on itself, the boards covered
with thick moss. Jimson and nightshade grew around the old
foundation. I walked through the chokecherry bushes to the
river and looked down into the cold waters of a backpool.
Two heavy-bellied bass stood in the clear water on wimpling
fins. I dropped a small clod of earth into the water and

watched them waggle slowly out into the deep part of the river. I turned and walked back to the house. An old wasp nest hung in one corner of the old house. Weeds grew high around the back. The house was all that remained of the original homestead started by my great-grandfather, Adam McCaslin, back at the turn of the century. The McCaslins have worked that land ever since. My grandfather, Juris, had expanded the original holding during World War I until our ranch covered nearly four thousand acres. When Pa was ten, Grandpa Juris moved the home place further north to take advantage of the newly graveled Bad River Road that the highway department had built to connect Wendte, Van Metre, Capa, Ithaca, and Midland in Haakon County, where I was born. The cabin only had two rooms to it, and the roof had pretty much fallen in on them. The sun and wind and rain had bleached the wood past gray into silver, but a weather vane still swung slowly from the roof peak, where two timbers crossed against a blue sky. The beak of the rooster on top of the vane was slightly askew where someone had dented it with a .22-caliber rifle, and his sides were feathered with rust, but he still turned creakingly with the wind and seemed to flaunt his tail feathers defiantly at the world. Nettles grew in what was once the yard, along with tall shoots of sourdock and shepherd's club and tickweed that Abel Six Feathers would occasionally gather and take home to his grandfather on the Pine Ridge Indian Reservation to the southwest after he came up to put in a few days working for Pa now and then.

Abel was there when I stepped into the clearing, and he looked up, his bronze face wreathed in a smile when he noticed the milk pail in my hand.

"Howdy, Sam. I see Samantha has you out choring for her," he said by way of greeting. I was named after Mom— the name that was her baptismal name and would one day appear on her granite-and-mica tombstone. I even looked like her with a spattering of freckles across the bridge of my nose and the auburn hair I kept clipped short. I was as rangy as rawhide bone and refused to be called "Samantha." A few days before, a couple of boys in Ithaca tried to treat me like a girl, but Johnny Stone popped one on the mouth when he made an indecent suggestion and the other I booted between his legs, sorta ruining his day. After that, the boys either ignored or tolerated me. Pa just took to it naturally. Mom finally gave up after a halfhearted attempt to make everyone call me by my full name. I think Pa secretly wanted a boy anyway. For the moment, I was annoyed at finding Abel there when I wanted privacy. Then I worried that he might tease me about this some day in Ithaca.

"Yeah," I grunted. I hefted the pail distastefully. "I thought I was going after some bass over at Harper's Pond, but I got fooled."

His smile broadened, and he turned to dig out another root of ragged cup with his knife. I admired it: a yellow-handled Stockman knife with a tiny black crack running down from the shield like a spider's web. He had been gathering for a while. A small pile of gravelroot lay on a ten-pound flour sack beside him along with some late-coming fireweed. "Yeah. It's a bad thing when a person's life ain't his own."

"Uh-huh. I don't know why she can't do this sort of thing herself. Women's work." I spat.

His teeth flashed as he smiled. "Don't worry," he said

laughing. His teeth flashed white, and I hoped I would have teeth like that when I was his age. "I won't tell."

I sighed inwardly, feeling safe. Abel Six Feathers' word was as good as the sunshine, Pa always said, and I reckoned he was right, for I never knew him to be wrong in sizing up a person. Ed Travers up in Pierre found that out when he tried to sell a small used '49 Ford tractor to Pa for nearly twice what he had given in trade to Oly Johnson. But Pa had talked with Oly before we went into town and knew that Oly had been having a lot of trouble with its choke before he turned it over in trade to the Allis Chalmers dealer. That was the last time Pa ever had any dealings with Ed Travers, as he moved his business over to the International Harvester people. Most people wouldn't have taken Abel's word for anything simply 'cause he was an Indian, but I never took much truck with those people. I guess I took after Pa in that matter.

"You going back home now that the branding's finished?" I asked.

He nodded. "Yep. Thought I would swing over here to the old homestead and pick up a few things for ol' Hump"—his grandfather, a Hunkpapa Sioux medicine man—"before I cut south. Hope you don't mind."

"I don't mind," I said. "Far as I know, we ain't got any use for that stuff."

"Most white folk don't," he said. But there was no rancor in his voice, just a plain stating of fact that acknowledged the differences between the two of us that both of us knew would always be there.

Fact is that society was pretty much divided three ways back then: the cowboys, the dam workers building the Oahe Dam outside of Fort Pierre, and the Indians. Back then, everyone

went into town Saturday afternoons to visit. Sometimes, there
was a dance at the old dance hall below the bluff in Fort Pierre
when the foothills cast long, still shadows across the town.
Then the cowboys and the dam workers would go across the
street to the Hop Scotch Bar, or down to the Snake Pit (that
wasn't its name, but I never heard it called anything else) on
the corner, or to the Silver Dollar Bar across the corner from
that to do their drinking. About midnight, all hell would
break loose, and fights would sometimes spill out into the
street and the police would come and break them up. The
Indians weren't welcome in the bars but bought their liquor
from the Chetek Liquor Store halfway between the Hop
Scotch and the Snake Pit and would sit in their old rusted-
out cars or on the gutter and quietly drink and talk among
themselves in the grunts and clicks and snaps of their own
language.

Some of the women would go out behind the Snake Pit
with the dam workers or cowboys down to where the Bad
River emptied into the Missouri River. The Indians parked
their cars there beneath the towering cottonwoods. We knew
what was going on in the backseats of those old cars that
rocked and squeaked on their ancient springs, and we often
hid out in the willows and laughed quietly among ourselves
as we watched to see who came "down to the river." Once,
we were watching when Tubby Watson stepped into this old
'38 Ford with Olive Yellow Eyes and when we saw his thin
shanks pistoning up and down, Stinky Porter flipped a cherry
bomb under the car. When it went off, Tubby tried to leap
up, banging his butt against the horn, but Olive had wrapped
her legs around his waist, holding him down, and damned if
that wasn't enough to give Tubby a rupture. He had a hard

time living that one down. He hurt so bad that he couldn't crawl off Olive Yellow Eyes, and the ambulance people had a hard time prying him out of that front seat, what with all the gawkers standing around and getting a fine eyeful of Olive Yellow Eyes' charms. And she wasn't bad-looking, save for a missing front tooth that someone had knocked out, leaving her lips fairly puffy.

Johnny Stone told me later that all of the boys came to know her pretty well a few years later when they finally figured out that sap-rising stuff Stocker talked about. She was quiet and gentle and kept their secrets from everyone. But I suspect that was just good business practice. Johnny used to say she could sell ice cubes to Eskimos, and maybe she could. Ed Preston kept her on at his hardware store despite complaints from the Baptist folks spouting gospel from their empty throats, because his business near doubled after he hired her.

Sometimes I would stay over the weekend at Grandma and Grandpa's house in Fort Pierre, and on Monday mornings I would go down to the courthouse with Bobby Buchanon and we'd join the others and watch as Jack Frost, the sheriff of Stanley County, led the Saturday-night fighters out from the basement jail for court. We could pretty much tell who had won by the pieces of sticking plaster and the scrapes and bruises. Of course, we always cheered for the cowboys, and sometimes, when some of the kids who belonged to the dam workers came down, the boys'd get into their own mock brawls and one of the deputies would run out and split them up, scattering everyone home. It always bothered me that the boys would avoid me at such times and that Johnny Stone kept himself close beside me when the dam boys would start their pushing and shoving. Once, however, I smacked one of those boys clean on his nose, and blood splattered all over his face and shirt and he took off for home, bawling like a new-born calf. Johnny yanked me out of that scuffle, though, and said something about how I needed to start acting like a girl *occasionally* at least. My temper flared and I almost pasted him one, but a freckle-faced kid beat me to it.

"You gonna be in town for the Thanksgiving Day Dance over at Ithaca?" I asked Abel.

He sat back on his heels and pushed his hat back with a knuckle. "Yep," he said. "It's been a while since the wife and kids got in off the reservation—except for the powwow over at White River, and that really don't count. Can't stay, though. My cousin Pete Stepping Wolf needs some help over at Wall with some horses. So, we'll probably go over there, then come back through Pierre for the Pearl Harbor Day sales. That'll give us some time to do a bit of Christmas shopping in Pierre before the snows come." He winked. "The kids have their orders in to Santa Claus already. How about you?"

"Naw," I said, scuffing the toe of my boot in the carpet of dead leaves. "There ain't no such thing as Santa Claus. It's okay for the kids to believe, though," I added hastily so as not to offend him.

He laughed. "Don't lose your faith in magic, Sam," he said. "There's time enough for that when you're older. What about you and your parents? You all going in?"

"Yeah. We're going into Fort Pierre first. Then we'll come back out to Ithaca. We always have Sunday dinner at Grandma's place," I said. "My uncle and aunt will be down from Belle Fourche this time, and Mom and Pa's cousins will be there, too, from up around Rapid City and Midland."

"Nice to have family around," he said.

"We do the same thing at Christmas," I added. "You guys do so, too?"

"Indians, you mean?" he asked, a tiny grin lifting his lips. I flushed. I could tell I was being teased, but I knew there was seriousness behind that teasing, too.

"I didn't mean nothing," I said, biting my lip. My face burned and I scuffed the toe of my boot against a clump of grama grass.

"I know," he said. He slipped the roots he had dug into the flour sack and rose. "But you can't help being you any more than I can help being me. My father was a white man. So I guess you could call me a half-breed. It's pretty hard living in two different worlds, neither one wanting you. But you play the hand you're dealt." He grinned. "Actually, it's better on the reservation for people like me. For the most part. My mother's people treat me pretty good."

"I didn't know that," I said.

"No reason for you to know it," he said. He frowned a little and added, "Don't know why I told you, either."

"But your name—"

"Why am I called Six Feathers?" I nodded. "I don't know who my father was. Mother won't say. I was raised by her parents. And they ain't talking, either. Of course, I don't see them often. They live up in the hills above Wounded Knee over in Pine Ridge. They don't have much to do with anyone who steps out of their world. Don't even have running water. They did their best with me, though." He frowned. "But there's always the time when you have to come in from the past. I wish I knew about my father, though." He shrugged. "He's probably dead now, I guess."

"That must be hard, not knowing," I said.

"You get over it. And if you look at it the right way, why, you get the best of both worlds."

He walked to his buckskin tied to a small willow by the creek. "Yeah, we celebrate Christmas, too. Best way we can, anyway. It's good for the kids to have something to look forward to. Sarah and Tommy sure like Christmas." He smiled. "And Anna and I do, too." He stepped into the stirrups and eased back into the saddle. He looked down at me and grinned again. "Tell your daddy that I'm grateful he thought of me for the fall branding. That'll handle Christmas for us. Otherwise"—he frowned—"we wouldn't have had much of one. Things are tight on the reservation thanks to Dillon Myer."

I nodded, remembering how Grandpa had nearly exploded when he read in the newspaper about how Eisenhower's man had tried to cut back on moneys for Indians living on reservations with a termination plan pushing them to move into cities. But the Indians had not been taught how to live in an industrial society, and they starved from loneliness and despair when they discovered they could not afford medical treatment and were given the worst jobs by the trade unions.

Abel lifted his hand and waved good-bye and nudged the buckskin with his heels. I watched as he rode out of sight. I sighed and shook my head. Grown-up things were hard to understand. I turned and walked behind the old house to a large stand of wild roses and bittersweet. The berries shone red and yellow, and I drew a deep breath, smelling the tang, then stepped in carefully among the bushes, trying to avoid the stickers and thorns.

Chapter II

"More pheasant?" Grandma Buttram—Ilsa—asked, holding the platter in front of me. I groaned inwardly.

"No, thanks, Grandma," I said politely. "I'm full."

She frowned and I sighed, knowing what was coming next. "Are you sure you're all right?" She looked at Mom. "She doesn't eat enough to keep a bird alive."

"I think she did all right," Grandpa Wolfgang interjected, looking critically at the plate in front of me with its smear of brown gravy, a blob of butter, and a red circle where I had piled the jellied cranberries. I looked at him gratefully and he winked. "Fact is, I think a piece of pumpkin pie and whipped cream will probably top off those mashed potatoes and yams and the venison and pheasant just right."

"Cake," I muttered.

"Cake," he said cheerfully. He snapped his fingers. "I forgot. Birthday cake." He shook his head in mock sorrow, teasing. "Sonofagun. You are another year older, today. How could I forget that? How old are you now? Eight?"

"Twelve," I said impatiently. "You know that."

"Hm. Yes, I guess I do. Well, that's what happens when you get old. You begin to forget things. I stand corrected." He patted his lips with his napkin and elaborately folded it and laid it beside his plate. His eyes twinkled. "Well, then, if everybody's ready, let's have some cake. All through?" He glanced around the table and made to rise.

"I'll have some more, please," my cousin Rose Marie said from across me, interrupting. She patted her hair—long and wavy, the color of orange poppies—and smirked at me. I made a face. I knew she was jealous, although her birthday had been the week before and we had all traipsed out to Rapid City in the Black Hills for it. She tossed her golden curls back and looked down her nose at me. "I think everything is just delicious."

Well, she was right there: everything was delicious. I looked down the board with its centerpiece of white Christmas roses—like massed funeral flowers—and noted the huge platters of venison and pheasant gathered from Grandpa's hunting trips to the Black Hills and the milo fields east of Pierre. Since his retirement from the Chicago & Northwestern Railroad, Grandpa had contented himself with his fishing rods and guns, and since I didn't shudder and squeal about stringing a worm on a hook, I was a frequent traveler with him whenever he could finagle a way to get me out of school. But no matter how clever he was, everyone could see through his ruses.

Once that fall, he had appeared outside the door to my classroom, twisting his gray fedora around in his huge hands and looking apologetically at Miss Miller, one of my teachers, as he explained to her that he sure hated to take me out of class and all, but this was an emergency and such. I groaned inwardly as my classmates looked at me curiously and Miss Miller fixed me with that steely look that belongs to spinster teachers who have been teaching a hundred years or so and have heard everything. I just knew she was going to make life miserable for me. I just knew it. Then, she took my coat from the closet and handed it to me and led me to the door, saying loudly that she certainly hoped the emergency wasn't too serious. We were halfway down the hall when she called to us and came over and bent down to stare at me. She winked solemnly and said, "Catch a good one for me." Then, she rose, nodded at Grandpa, and marched back to her classroom, leaving the two of us staring open-mouthed at her back.

"Now that is one smart teacher," Grandpa muttered to me. "We need more like her." I fervently agreed. But, I wanted to add, we needed more like Grandpa, too, who knew education wasn't limited to the classroom.

"Isn't she a wonderful girl?" Aunt Flo, Rose Marie's mother, beamed at her. Rose Marie simpered and daintily patted her lips with her napkin. "Just a precious little thing."

I looked at Grandpa. His iron-gray eyebrow twitched, and I knew what he was thinking. I shook my head. Aunt Flo caught the movement and sniffed.

"It wouldn't hurt for some others to learn a few manners *and* how young ladies should behave," she said.

"She's just not hungry," Pa said quietly. "Doesn't have anything to do with manners. Has to do with appetite." Pa had a hard time stomaching Aunt Flo and the airs she put on after scouring issues of *Vogue.* But he pretty much kept his mouth shut to preserve a little peace in the family. I could tell, though, when he was approaching his limit because he'd get tight little wrinkles around the corners of his eyes, and when his lips turned down and the bottom one disappeared in a tight line, it was best to leave him alone. The white lines were beginning to appear.

"Well, I don't eat between meals. Leastways, not like some," Rose Marie said, flouncing her hair around and patting her curls and sticking her nose up in the air like she smelled something rank around her. I knew what her problem was, though. She had come into the living room before dinner just as I had taken the last piece of pink wintergreen candy—her favorite—from the cut-glass dish and popped it into my mouth.

I couldn't help myself. "Oink, oink," I said. Grandpa coughed and hurriedly reached for his coffee cup. Pa lifted his napkin and busied himself wiping his lips.

"Samantha!" Mom said sternly. Her eyes snapped angrily at me. "That's not nice!"

"Sorry," I mumbled. I looked at Rose Marie, who stared at me as if she was going to cry.

"Well! I think I know someone who's going to get coal in her slippers instead of presents this Christmas," Aunt Flo said grimly. I looked at Uncle Jimmy, her husband. He looked embarrassed and busied himself with another serving of cranberry salad. Rose Marie was an only child like me and Aunt Flo had high aspirations for her. She bought Rose Marie's clothes from mail-order catalogs with names like Neiman Marcus and Saks and such and twice a year—once in the spring and again in the fall—took Rose Marie to Chicago to buy clothes and experience cultural enrichment, whatever that meant. Uncle Jimmy was a mining engineer and taught at the School of Mines in Rapid City and let Aunt Flo do pretty much what she wanted even if he didn't like it.

"It is Sam's birthday," Grandpa said mildly. "I think we can cut her a bit of slack."

"Birthday or not—" Aunt Flo began, but Grandpa broke in.

"And speaking of such, I think it's time for presents. Then

we can have the cake and ice cream, don't you think?"

"Well," Aunt Flo began, her lips pursing primly like she had sucked too long on a lemon drop.

"Don't you think?" Grandpa asked, staring steadily at Aunt Flo. I recognized the edge to his voice that suggested no one wanted to argue further. Aunt Flo seemed to wilt at that and picked up her cup of coffee and drank from it, her little pinkie extended as rigid as a bone. She lapsed into silence, and Grandpa smiled and slapped the table with his meaty hand.

"Good! Now, let's all go into the sitting room and see what kinda loot this gal has come up with! Then, we'll have the cake and—"

"I'm not finished yet," Rose Marie complained. She speared a French-cut bean with her fork and carried it to her mouth, chewing slowly. She stared mockingly at me, and I knew she was going to dawdle as long as possible to keep me at the table.

I pushed my chair back from the table, avoiding Mom's eye, knowing that I'd get a lecture on manners when we headed back to Ithaca. Suddenly a pall seemed to be cast over the day, and I looked at Rose Marie, who swallowed with exaggerated effort, then pretended to search for the right bean before she speared it with her fork, examined it again, then carried it to her mouth, chewing slowly.

"Momma says you should chew each bite thirty times before swallowing," she said primly.

I looked at the heap of food remaining on her plate and calculated by that reasoning she had a good two hours of chewing left ahead of her.

"Excuse me," I said politely. "I have to go to the bathroom. Don't wear out your teeth," I added. "You might have to gum your cake."

I left the table without waiting for permission and walked through the kitchen and into the bathroom, shutting the door behind me. I sat on the toilet lid and propped my chin in my hands, resting my elbows on my knees. I stared out the window at the mat of grapevines crawling through the chicken wire strung along the porch that ran down one side of the old railroad house. It was the same old story. Every time we got together, I got into trouble with Rose Marie. Despite every promise I made to myself that I would ignore her, she managed to do something to get under my skin and draw Mom's wrath down upon my shoulders. There was just something about Rose Marie that made me forget all my good intentions. At the time I thought she was mentally defective, but she was only spoiled rotten, being an only child—like me.

"You need to tolerate her, Samantha," Mom said time and time again. "She is a nice little girl and you could learn from that. I know she irritates you, but remember that it is the Christian thing to do."

Somehow I didn't think that Jesus Christ had spoiled girl cousins in mind when He admonished us to turn the other cheek, but I knew better than to argue theology with Mom. She had read the Bible from cover to cover and still read it every night for a half hour before going to bed while Pa sat in his easy chair reading *The Stockman*. Although Pa had little truck with her Methodist ways, he didn't say anything on Sunday when Mom dressed herself and me in church clothes and headed toward the little brown-and red-bricked Welsh Methodist Church six miles out from Ithaca. The minister,

Reverend John T. Boskins, would rant and rave while he recalled the sufferings of Jesus and how Satan lured the mortals into his lair. "He is legion!" he shouted at the top of his lungs. And I asked him one day in Sunday school if I was a figment of God's imagination or if He was a figment of mine. The good reverend told Mom, and Mom promptly grounded me for three weeks.

Pa wasn't a heretic; he believed in God and Jesus Christ, but he reckoned as to how they probably had enough on their hands elsewhere with those who couldn't do for themselves that they didn't need him horning in and demanding favors from them or telling them how to do their jobs. To Pa's way of thinking, man had his responsibilities and God had His, and things would be a whole lot better if others would cut each a little slack and let the reins down a bit so a person could work at what needed to be done. So Pa left the Methodists pretty much alone, and they left him alone, although they whispered behind Mom's back when she walked into Sunday services, trailing me reluctantly behind her. Sometimes the words rattled a little too loudly, and Mom would turn around and calmly stare at them until a deep flush came up their scrawny throats and turned their leathery cheeks bronze.

The minister took Pa's attitude in stride and came out once a month or so to try and convert him from his heathen ways, but I sorta had the idea that he liked Pa's independence and Pa tolerated him—more for the sake of Mom than for his liking of the turnings and twistings of the reverend's maundering ways with Scripture. Still, it was a lot different from the Baptist Church and Reverend Larry Flynn, who got himself so worked up spouting his tomfoolery that he'd slobber onto his black suit, spraying the front two rows of his holy-rolling parishioners, who waxed gleefully in his words as if they had been rebaptized with holy fire and brimstone. Reverend Flynn had little use for Pa, and Pa had even less use for him, dismissing him with a few words that cast little doubt as to his opinion of people who had no tolerance for another's idea, like Flynn, who was dead certain that only a select few would earn God's grace come Judgment Day. But I reckoned that to be just Baptists in general, because every one I've ever run up against always had a rather narrow view of what was right and wrong—and that changed pretty regularly according to what they needed at the moment. Pa always said that the Lord created other religions so He would have an ace-in-the-hole if a stinker came along as they did when the Baptists came.

"Samantha! You come out of there," Mom said furiously through the door, breaking into my thoughts.

I sighed and flushed the toilet and walked out of the bathroom. Mom's eyes were flinty, but tiny nerves twitched around them. Her lips were drawn down into a thin line.

"I'm not going to ask you to apologize to Rose Marie, Samantha. But I want you to think about how you hurt her. And to help you out with that, I think we'll just load up your presents and take them back to the ranch with us, and you can have them later when you decide you're sorry."

"I'm sorry right now," I mumbled, looking away from her angry eyes.

She shook her head vehemently. "Oh, no. You're not getting out of this that easy, young lady. You just hop back in there and tell Rose Marie how sorry you are, and we'll let you think about it for a few days." She took a sudden deep breath and pressed her fingers against her stomach as if she was in pain. Her face tightened, deep lines digging themselves in around her cheeks. She pointed a finger toward the dining room.

"Yes, ma'am." I sighed. I crossed the kitchen back into the dining room, dragging my heels as I went. It wasn't fair, I wanted to tell her. Rose Marie was doing that purposefully with her pretended eating habits. But I knew Mom would just repeat what she'd said about me having to be tolerant and all.

They all still sat around the table. Pa's lips quivered, but his eyes were stern behind his steel-rimmed glasses. Grandpa poured a little coffee into his saucer and blew on it, sipping. Aunt Flo sniffed and glared at me while Uncle Jimmy sighed and pulled at his long nose as if he wanted to rearrange it on his face. Grandma was mad—I didn't have to look at her to know that. I could feel her anger, as righteous as Billy Sunday's, pouring over the table at me. Rose Marie was the type of granddaughter Grandma thought she should have. I was an accident of nature—I'd overheard her say that once to Aunt Flo when she thought Mom and me had left the house when we hadn't and the door to the porch was standing wide open. I knew she'd never say nothing to deliberately hurt me, but a person can't help what they're feeling and sometimes those feelings just verbalize themselves. Pa says it's like running off at the mouth before putting the brain in gear. Sometimes growing up becomes so complicated. Rose Marie just stared at me, her blue eyes deep in the baby fat that still hung around her high cheekbones.

"I'm sorry, Rose Marie," I said. "I didn't mean to hurt your feelings."

"Well, you did! You always hurt me!" she said. Tears

welled up in her eyes, threatening to spill over her cheeks. I knew I was in big trouble. Rose Marie could turn on the faucets at the drop of a rouge brush if she wanted, and it always seemed to me that I was hard put to keep my head above those floodwaters.

I sighed and shrugged, not knowing what else to say.

Grandpa cleared his throat. "Well, that's over and done with. Let's go into the sitting room and get on with the day."

"I don't think so," Mom said. She reached for her coffee cup, her knuckles showing white from her anger. Her eyes had stubbornly lowered themselves half-shut so that milky crescents showed. "I think Samantha needs a lesson."

"It's her birthday," Grandpa said gently. "You can afford a little forgiveness, too. Practice what you preach." He stared at Aunt Flo. "Fact is, I think others around here could use a few lessons in manners as well." Aunt Flo blushed red and opened her mouth to speak, but Grandpa turned pointedly away from her, ignoring Grandma, who looked like she was about to explode, and stared at Mom. But Mom's chin rose, and I knew the issue was settled. So much for my birthday.

Grandpa shook his iron-gray head and picked up and dropped his napkin by his plate, rising. He stared at Mom and said, "I think you're making a mountain out of a molehill here. Kids can't help being kids and you gotta let them grow up by themselves at times. You can't lead them into being grown-up with a ring through their noses. That's like leading a prize bull calf around a sale ring. You gotta give them a little room and let them make their mistakes."

"Well, she just made one," Mom said, sniffing.

"Yeah," Grandpa answered. "But do *you* know why?" He glanced at Rose Marie, glanced pointedly at her plate, and shook his head. "I'd say she had a little help along the way. There's more than one kind of cruelty and some kids learn real young how to use them all." He looked again at Aunt Flo. "Mendacity!" he snorted, and shuffled away from the table, and the day seemed to slip into gray and gloom.

Rose Marie pushed her plate away from her and said, "Well, can I have some cake, now?"

"Maybe," Uncle Jimmy said, clearing his throat. "Maybe we could all use a piece."

"Thank you, but I'm full," I said quietly. I looked steadily at Rose Marie. "You can have my piece, too. I wouldn't want you to get too peckish. You might not fit into them fancy ruffles anymore."

Mom's lips tightened, but suddenly I didn't care. The day was ruined, and a piece of cake wasn't going to make it suddenly seem bright and fun again. I rose and followed Grandpa into the sitting room, where he carefully rolled an after-dinner cigarette from a red tin of Eagle Claw tobacco and lit it with a kitchen match. He blew the match out and dropped it into a pink ashtray with NIAGARA FALLS 1992 written in gold around the base. He sighed and picked up his newspaper and opened it, and began reading about the troops still in Korea.

A murmur of low voices came from the dining room, and I could hear Uncle Jimmy arguing halfheartedly that allowances should be made for me because it was my birthday, but I knew that look on Mom's face and knew the more she was pushed, the stubborner she'd become. I gave up and slipped into my jean jacket and went outside. I walked down the boardwalk to an old box elder tree that hung over the parking lot and dirt street. Grandpa's green '53 Chevrolet was parked under it, and I crawled up into a wide fork that let me sprawl out over the roof of the car. I stared across the street to the huge three-story house surrounded by thick lilac bushes where Janie Taylor lived and wished she was home and not visiting with her uncles and aunts south of Pierre.

Janie's mother had been real sick the past summer and lost all of her hair. She took to wandering around the neighborhood and down to the river, mumbling to herself, her fingers pulling at her lips. Occasionally she'd stop in the middle of the street, clench her fists, and shake them at the heavens while shouting, "Why me? Why me?" Once she took off her clothes and ran through the streets, yelling, "Blessed be! Blessed be!" It took folks the better part of the day to catch her, and afterward I heard one of the men say something about how she could have given lessons to the high school quarterback on how to avoid tackles. Every once in a while she'd come out of whatever world she was in and bake up a mess of gingerbread cookies, but as the months rolled on, the cookie batches came fewer and fewer. Then they stopped coming altogether, and she spent all her days sitting in the bay window in her living room, staring out at the lilac bushes. In the fall, when Toby, Janie's father, was out to the ranch helping bring in a late hay cutting, her mother took a double-barreled shotgun from Toby's den, drove in her green Buick to the top of the shale hills overlooking Fort Pierre where the Verendyre monument stood, and blew her brains out.

The door opened, and I turned my head and watched as Grandpa shuffled out of the house in his Congress boots, pulling a light jacket over his black-and-white-checked flannel shirt tucked into gray trousers. He wore his gray fedora hat pulled down low to his steel-gray eyebrows. He ambled down to the box elder tree and leaned against it while he lit another of his hand-rolled cigarettes. I remembered the set-to he and Grandma had had when word shot like wildfire around the neighborhood about Janie's mom.

"Ain't gonna be much of a Christmas over there," Grandpa had said, clicking his tongue against his front teeth and shaking his head. "Best thing that could be done would have been to let her go when the chance was there instead of trying to bring her around so many times."

"That ain't a decision for you to make," Grandma had snapped. "Ain't a decision for no one but God. And I think you would know that more if you attended church a few more times instead of sitting on the bank with a fishing pole."

"Which church would you like me to go to?" Grandpa had asked, and Grandma flushed and let him be. Grandpa had been raised Catholic, and when Grandma wouldn't come into that church, he'd married her in Van Metre when Presbyterian Reverend Peter Smiley came out from Fort Pierre on the section line dumpie towed behind the motorcar to visit the folks there and to have a beer or two away from his flock. He married Grandma and Grandpa in Nordquist's store. Grandpa promptly proclaimed himself satisfied, refusing to go through the Methodist offices when Grandma's parents suggested it might be the thing to do. Later, I heard how Grandma's folks took a dim view of Grandpa when he'd opened up his toolshed where he'd stored a bit of 'shine from Old Man Ferris's still and gotten Reverend Smiley so drunk that he sat on the steps to Nordquist's store, singing "Auld Lang Syne" over and over until Grandma's older brother Heinie threatened to whack him over his head and put him out of his misery. As I heard it from Stocker, who got it from Old Man Ferris, Reverend Smiley drew himself up, punched out

Grandma's brother, then pitched forward into the dust, sawing logs.

But, I reflected, staring across at the huge house, Grandpa had been right: it wasn't going to be a good Christmas for Janie and her father this year.

Around about four that afternoon, we all piled into our automobiles and headed back to Midland for the Thanksgiving Day Dance. I held out to ride with Grandpa and Grandma, which brought about a whining complaint from Rose Marie that she, too, wanted to ride with them. And although Grandpa really didn't want her along, he kept his mouth shut. As a result, Rose Marie and I rode in the backseat together while Pa rode with Uncle Jimmy and Mom drove Aunt Flo, who complained loudly that she hadn't quite gotten the hang of that automatic transmission, yet. "Honest, I keep hitting the brake with my left foot when I try to shift!" she complained. "It is just so difficult!" Then she blushed when Grandpa dryly allowed that was a problem when one didn't know Gee from Haw.

Aunt Flo and Uncle Jimmy were going to stay with us on the ranch after the dance as then they would be halfway home to Rapid City, while Grandma and Grandpa were going to spend the night in Capa with Fred and Alice Buchanon, old friends from the days when Grandpa used to run the section house on the Chicago & Northwestern and the Denver & Rio Grande shared the track line up to the Pierre roundhouse.

I wasn't looking forward to the dance or to letting Rose Marie share my room. I had offered to bunk in with Stocker in the bunkhouse, but Mom would hear nothing about that. She said something about proprieties, but I couldn't catch her meaning. Resentment ran deep on sharing my bed, but I was already in enough hot water with Mom so I kept my lip buttoned tight and pretended that I didn't care a whit one way or the other about the arrangements, while reminding myself to use the old skeleton key to lock my closet door against Rose Marie's prying. I knew that would miff her more, but she wouldn't be able to say anything about it because then she would be scolded for being a snoop, although she was the snoopingest person I ever knew with the possible exception of Reverend Flynn, who looked so hard to find another's misdoings that he plumb passed over their good sides.

We pulled into Midland behind a caravan of gypsies who came down Cemetery Hill in solemn procession, their old black cars geared low and pulling round silver trailers. At the bottom of the hill, they turned right into Jacob's Field and cut across the broomstraw to the cottonwoods by the river, where they were allowed to park their trailers and put up their carny tents. It was kinda late in the season for the gypsies as they usually came in late fall to tease us into skipping school and wandering around their camp. As outcasts from the rest of society they carried a hint of the exotic and danger with them in their colorful costumes, swarthy skins, and wild music. I had never seen a man wear an earring before like their leader and thought that was just grand and daring. They were tolerated, but Reverend Flynn always made certain that he warned his flock against their thieving ways and to guard the children from being kidnapped by the children of Canaan who had been cursed by Moses for their evil ways. I suppose there was something to that, because folks claimed a gypsy would steal anything that wasn't tied or glued down. I never saw any of them do anything like that, though, and when I got the chance to walk through their camp, they all treated me nice and one woman told my fortune for free by looking into this glass ball and claiming she could see the future. I looked mighty hard but all I could see were tiny pricks of lights and a small shadow in the center. The old woman said I had to be very careful because great danger was coming in the snow. But the sky was as blue as a cornflower then and the sun hot enough on the back of my neck that a trickle of sweat was running down my back. So I figured she was just leading me on some and let it go at that. I thanked her and said I'd keep an eye out for trouble, and she smiled and said I was a good girl with a strong heart and gave me a piece of toffee candy she'd made. She must have said something to the king or whatever he was—an old man who looked as wrinkled as Methuselah—because he stopped me later and pressed a little token in my hand, a silver medal that had a face in the center supported by three legs bent at the knee. He said I should wear it always to guard against the Evil Eye, and the way he whispered those last two words made my flesh go all pebbly. I put it on a chain and hung it around my neck and tucked under my shirt.

We arrived at the dance hall about the same time that Johnny Stone's parents pulled in, and I waved at him as we walked inside, bringing a curl to Rose Marie's lip.

"Is that your boyfriend?" she asked loudly.

My ears grew warm as Mom looked around and saw the Stones standing beside the small stage where the musicians sat on wooden folding chairs, teetering back and forth, laughing and joking among themselves as they tuned their instruments. The fat man with the guitar (Harold Stroyer) laughed and said something to Melvin Peebles, who turned a fiddle peg and spread his lips up from his toothless gums as he grinned at Stroyer's joke. A wasp passed through the laddered light behind him and disappeared up among the rafters. Mom waved at Martha and glanced again at me, her eyes crinkling teasingly at the corners. My ears grew warm.

"Why don't you say it a little louder?" I said irritably. "There must be someone in Haakon County who didn't hear you."

The humor snapped away from Mom's eyes. "Samantha," Mom warned.

I shook my head, swallowing my anger. This sure wasn't my day anymore and I had Rose Marie to thank for that. I walked across the dance floor to where Johnny and some other friends stood with their backs against the wall, sucking on straws in small bottles of Coca-Cola by the stand where the Waldorfs sold bottles of pop and small sacks of potato chips and salted peanuts still in the shell and stale candy bars.

"Hey," Johnny said as I came up. He nodded over at Rose Marie. "Who's the girl with the big mouth?"

"My cousin," I grunted. "A royal pain." I took the bottle from his hand and drew a deep swallow, handing it back. "And you're welcome to her. Please."

His eyebrows raised. "Problems?"

"She just cost me my birthday, that's all," I said. "Spoiled rotten."

"Kinda cute, though," he said thoughtfully. "She dance?"

"According to her, she can do anything. I suppose that would include riding Midnight," I said, mentioning the then-world-champion horse who had thrown all his riders in rodeos around the state.

"Aw," Freddy Brown said. "Ain't nobody gonna ride Midnight. Not even Casey Tibbs."

Now, that was enough to finally put a damper on my day. Casey Tibbs was the World Champion Cowboy but more important than that, he was a friend. Why, just last year when they were putting in a showroom for all his trophies at the Falcon Café in Pierre, Pa had taken me in to meet him and he signed a picture of himself for me and told me that if he ever had a girl, he would give her my name. Besides, when he wasn't rodeoing around the country, he worked on his ranch, which was only twenty-some-odd miles from us. He came over to help with branding season sometimes. Pa had actually team-roped with him a couple of times before he and Mom married. Pa was the heeler.

Normally we let Freddy Brown have his way 'cause his mother had froze to death in a snowbank two years before when her car slid off the highway into the ditch between Hayes and Four Corners. She had tried to make it to a ranch house by following a lane that cut through a fence, but the snow was so thick that she lost her way and the men found her three days later six miles down south in a buffalo wash. They followed the ravens, who had followed the coyotes, and there wasn't much of her left to put in a casket by the time they got to her. But there were just some boundaries that a person couldn't allow another to cross, and coming down on Casey Tibbs was one of them.

"I guess Casey Tibbs could ride just about whatever it was he wanted to ride," I said pointedly. I shoved my hands into my pockets and stared at Freddy, giving him a chance to take back his sacrilegious words.

Paul Bluchard came to the microphone, bowing, pointing, and smiling, his booted feet tapping to the music. Tiny lights glinted from his huge belt buckle and from his tie slide in the shape of a bucking horse. His hair was well oiled and combed straight back off his high forehead.

"Howdy," he said in his warm baritone. "Get your partners and join your hands so you can tap your toes to our good band."

People laughed good-naturedly at his near-rhyme and moved around into their squares as he began his call:

"Here we go with the old chuck wagon.
Hind wheel's broke and axle's draggin'.
Meet your honey and pat her on the head."

Freddy grinned at the others and winked. "Of course he can—if he's sober enough to cinch on his saddle."

"Freddy," Johnny said warningly. He looked at my face and moved his feet uneasily. "Let it drop."

But Freddy had himself an audience by now. He looked around, savoring the moment. "Why, everybody knows that Casey Tibbs spends most of his time sucking whiskey at the Silver Dollar," Freddy said. He hooked a thumb in his wide leather belt and rocked back on his boot heels, grinning like an ape. He took a swig from his Coke bottle.

"Better take up a little slack in your lip, Porkface," I warned. My neck grew warm and everything seemed to grow bright and cold. Johnny moved uneasily and tried to draw me away. I shook off his hand.

"Or what?" Freddy sneered. He handed his Coca-Cola bottle to Johnny and placed his hands on his hips. "Well? You gonna fish or cut bait?"

"You don't fight girls, Freddy," Johnny said warningly. He tossed the half-full bottle into the trash can behind him.

"Hey! That was half-full!" Freddy objected.

"And?" Johnny said deliberately. He gave Freddy a shove in the chest with the flat of his hand. "You think I'm gonna stand and hold your stuff for you like a goddamned Indian?"

Freddy flushed and looked back at me. He refused to answer Johnny because he had a yellow streak near two hands wide running down his back. Fighting with girls wasn't all that popular around most of the country, but out in western South Dakota, girls grew up hard and had to hold their own until the men became interested in them otherwise—if they were lucky. There were a few like the Anderson sisters, Holly and Molly, who could split more firewood than a lot of men, shoot better than most, and were something fearsome when they had a drink or two at the Hop Scotch in Fort Pierre. Molly had cleaned out more than one tavern on the mile-section lines when a couple of cowboys got to poking at her with something a bit more than funning. So, although Freddy might get a bit of teasing, I had whipped my share of boys. And if the truth be told, because I was a girl I had it a bit better than them, 'cause most boys were reluctant to throw a punch and more than likely wanted to take me down to the ground and hold me there until I cooled off. Johnny was about the only one who had managed that, and more than once I had blackened his eye and cut his lip before he could. I could tell from the way Freddy looked at me that he thought he might make a case for himself by bringing a fight up between us, then backing off because I was a girl and it wouldn't do for him to dust his hands with a pint-size like me. He was bigger—fatter, anyway; he didn't have the nickname Porkface for nothing—and he could get away from an actual fight because I was a girl. "If you weren't a girl—"

He grunted as Johnny gave him another push, this time lower, catching him just below the breastbone. "But she is a girl. You taking to fighting girls now?"

The others around us began to laugh. Freddy flushed and shook a warning finger at Johnny. "This ain't between you and me. It's between me and her. She wants to wear man's pants, then she can take what a man takes."

"And what about you?" Johnny said, stepping deliberately closer to him. "You're wearing man's pants."

"Knock it off, Johnny," I said. "I can handle my own problems—especially a fat tub of guts like this one."

"Who do you calling a tub of guts?" Freddy demanded, trying to step around Johnny. But Johnny moved with him and he trod on Johnny's foot. Johnny gave him a shove that staggered him backward.

"Who do you think you are, stepping on my foot like that?" Johnny demanded.

"This is enough. Let's take it outside," I said, jerking my thumb.

"I dunno," Freddy said, glancing nervously around at the adults. But they paid no attention to us, the men swinging their girls around as fast as they could, trying to get their dresses to flare up past their garters. The women shrieked, and some of them let their dresses flare up as high as they would go. But I wasn't interested in a quick look at white thighs and Sara Larkin's red ruffled panties that she took great pride in showing off to all and sundry who might be watching on the dance floor—as long as her husband, brother, or father wasn't around and they were usually out among the pickups having a snort or two. I never saw any family snorting as much as the Larkins did, but they had the worst land around and most of their water had an alkali taste to it that meant they had to test it regularly to keep it from becoming poisoned.

I turned and walked from the dance hall.

Outside, the air had a crisp feel to it and the water standing in the tire tracks already had a thin skin of ice over it. A small group of men stood next to an old '38 Ford with its trunk open, passing a bottle of Old Crow whiskey back and forth. I recognized them—Ed Wilson and Tubby Watson and Earl and Leonard Byers. Tubby Watson once worked for us, until Pa caught him using a cattle prod on a horse that had crow-hopped and thrown him, and fired him. They laughed as they watched us pass and jostled each other.

"Looks like the first fight's ready to happen," Tubby Watson sniggered.

We ignored them and rounded a corner. I stopped and turned, facing Freddy as he came up to me. The others spread out around us in a circle.

"Well?" he taunted. He put his hands back on his hips and threw his head back, grinning down at me. "Whatcha gonna do now?"

Johnny stepped around in front of me and turned to face Freddy. "You're asking the wrong one, Freddy. Ask me."

"This is between—"

"I've heard that," Johnny said. "But you made it my business, now. So, what're you going to do?"

"Damnit, Johnny," I said angrily. He glanced over his shoulder at me.

"Stay out of this, Sam."

That did it. I'd had enough of folks pushing me around

on my birthday. I ignored him and stepped around his off-shoulder to Freddy's side.

"How tall are you?" I asked.

He frowned. "What's that got to do with anything?"

"I didn't know they piled it that high," I said, and swung from my heels, my fist cracking against his jaw.

"Goddamnit, Sam!" Johnny said loudly.

I ignored him and tried to step forward as Freddy staggered back from my blow, but Johnny grabbed my arm, spinning me half-around. Freddy would have fallen except the boys surrounding us caught him and threw him back toward me. He flailed his arms, his fists windmilling. One caught me high on the forehead, stunning me, and I knew a lump would form. I jerked away from Johnny, stepped to the side, and dug my fist deep into Freddy's stomach. Johnny grabbed me again as Freddy folded at the waist, gagging. Then he fell to his knees and wrapped his arms around my legs, pulling me down. Johnny fell on top of me. The air went out of my lungs with a *woof!* I rolled out from under Johnny. Freddy tried to squirm on top of me, but I rolled with him, smacking his nose with my elbow, bringing forth a howl of pain. I slipped away, still on my knees. Freddy started to swing at me. I ducked automatically, but Johnny caught Freddy's arm and hauled off, busting him in the mouth. His lips split and he cried out.

"Johnny—" I started angrily, but Freddy, enraged now, came toward me. He threw a punch. I ducked under it, then shoved myself forward from my knees, tackling him. I jerked my head up under his chin and heard his teeth click hard together. Then I felt someone pulling me off him.

"Here, now! Stop this!" a voice said.

I swiveled my head and recognized Abel Six Feathers. Behind him stood a pretty woman with long blond hair tied in a ponytail. She watched solemnly as Abel spread his arms, keeping us apart.

"Sam!" he said sharply. "Stop this! You too!" He shook Freddy by his shoulder. His head snapped back and forth. "Fighting don't settle anything!"

"Spoken like a true Injun," someone said sarcastically. "Ain't a one of them nervy enough to fight a man square on. Have to make like they wanna have peace with him and the minute he turns his back, they jump him. Seen it happen more than once down around Parmalee."

I craned my head and looked at Tubby Watson and the men who had been sharing the bottle of whiskey when we trooped past them minutes before. He spat to the side and stepped forward. "Leave 'em alone, Injun. This here don't concern you none."

"Maybe," Abel said. "But it should concern somebody." He looked down at me. "What do you think your mother and father would say, Sam?"

I shrugged.

"Don't matter none until they do say something," Tubby said. A wicked smile curled his thick lips. His yellow teeth stood out wolfishly. He was short—no, not short, but long in the waist and short-legged, as if his legs had been cut off at the knees. His head was shaped like a bullet, his hair close-cropped so his hat slipped down over his head and was held up off his nose by his ears that stuck out like bat wings. His eyes stared piggishly from the suety folds of his cheeks. His lips looked like pieces of liver hiding rabbit teeth. "What we don't need is some red nigger coming along and telling us that he's the one to say something." He looked around at the others standing beside him. Someone chuckled. "What the hell you doing here, anyways?"

"Figured on going to the dance," Abel said quietly. He pushed Freddy and me away and took a step, putting himself between his wife and the men.

"This here's a white man's dance," Tubby said. "You Injuns have your own powwows down on the reservation." He stretched his neck, looking around Abel at his wife. He nodded approvingly.

"Maybe," Abel said. His eyes went cold and a heavy blankness came over them.

The woman stepped forward, putting her hand on his arm. "Abel," she said softly, "we don't need this. Let's go home."

"Best listen to your squaw," Tubby said.

"Right pretty one," someone (I think it was Ed Wilson) said. "Maybe she'd like to dance out here. We could use the backseat of my Chevy."

"Now, that's a thought," Tubby said, grinning. He wiped his nose with a thick nicotine-stained forefinger with a horn-like nail. "What you think about that? There's four of us. That should be enough to have a little party, don't you think? We got a bottle of whiskey and, well, I reckon we could scratch up a dollar or two apiece."

"I think you've said enough," Abel said quietly, sliding his wife behind him.

"Shit, it ain't talking that I'm about," Tubby said. He swaggered up to stand close beside Abel. He reached out and pushed Abel's shoulder.

Abel gave a tiny smile, turned as if to walk away, then

pivoted on his toes, swiveling his hips, and slugged Tubby on his jaw, knocking him backward to the ground.

"What the hell," Leonard began.

Tubby lifted himself up on his elbow, stuck a dirty fore-finger inside his mouth, and pulled out a tooth. He spat a mouthful of blood on the ground, then roared, climbed to his feet, and tried to swing at Abel. Abel jabbed with his left fist, snapping Tubby's head back, then crossed with his right, hit-ting Tubby high up on the eye.

Tubby's eyes crossed like he'd been cold-cocked with a frying pan. He reeled away, falling.

"Grab him!" someone yelled.

Ed Wilson took a step, then groaned and grabbed his groin, sinking to his knees as Abel's narrow-toed boot flashed up into his crotch. Abel slid away and caught Earl with a right. Tubby reached out and wrapped his arms around Abel's knees, throwing him off balance, and then the others swarmed over him.

I turned and ran into the dance hall, glanced around, and saw Pa standing quietly among a group of men, visiting. I ran up to him.

"Pa," I gasped. "A bunch of men have Abel down. They're beating him pretty badly."

Pa glanced at the men, then limped hurriedly from the dance hall. I led him around the corner. Three men held Abel while Tubby stood in front of him, his fist drawn back. It never landed. Pa stepped forward, grabbed his arm, and pulled him off balance, spinning him away. Others stepped in, pulling the men away from Abel. He sagged for a moment, then caught himself and stood up straight. He looked at me and nodded.

"Thanks, Sam," he said quietly.

Tubby stared at me murderously, then looked at Pa. "What you doing messing in this affair?" he asked.

Pa stared at him coldly. "Always looking for an edge, aren't you, Watson?"

"This ain't none of yours," Tubby said sullenly.

"I'm making it mine," Pa said quietly.

"You an Injun-lover now, McCaslin?" Tubby said.

Then his eyes rattled back and forth as he realized he'd gone a bit too far with his words. A man could get away with a lot of things, but there were a few that just automatically earned him a knuckle sandwich and calling a man an Injun-lover was one of the worst. The men automatically stepped back, giving them room. Pa's face looked like the time we caught a coyote eating at the gut of a cow that was mooing sharply in pain and mired deep in gumbo-mud so she hadn't been able to get out.

"I reckon that's no affair of yours, Watson," Pa said softly, but there was an edge to his words that made my stomach flip-flop. "But I'd expect nothing more from a man who'd been caught in the pig lot."

The men laughed at this. Even we kids got to smiling from the story we'd heard about Tubby being caught doing his strange ways. His face burned with shame and he looked like he wanted to say something, but he'd already shot enough word fodder in the air that still hung unresolved.

Pa nodded at Abel, who'd caught his breath by now and had moved up to stand beside Pa against the others. "You want to meet him fair and square?"

Tubby stared at Abel for a long moment, then turned on his heel and left. Some of the men laughed and someone shouted something about pigs after him, but I didn't catch it and when I asked Johnny about it later, he wouldn't tell me. The others avoided Pa's eyes and followed Tubby, Ed Wilson limping painfully, his legs bowed as if saddle-galled. Pa shook his head and stared at Abel. "I don't want to know what started this," he said. "I guess you had a good reason. But I would watch myself, if I were you. Watson's a mean one and a coward. That's a bad combination."

"Thank you, Mr. McCaslin," Abel said.

His wife stepped forward and took his arm. "Come," she said in a low voice. "Let's go home."

Abel shook his head. "We came to the dance. We're gonna dance. We have as much right here as anybody."

"I wouldn't argue that," Pa said. "The question is, though, is it worth it?"

"Ten minutes ago, I would have said no," Abel said. He took a handkerchief from his back pocket and wiped his face. "But now, I'd say yes."

Pa stared at Abel for a long minute, then nodded slowly and stretched out his hand. Abel shook it, then put his arm around the shoulders of his wife, hugging her to him. Tears glistened in her eyes, but for the life of me I couldn't figure out why, unless she was thankful that Abel hadn't been hurt.

Abel led her into the dance hall. Word of what had happened had already spread, and the others there gave them a wide berth when they walked down the floor to the end. The band broke into a dance, and Pa pulled Mom into a square with Abel and his wife and the four of them danced together for the rest of the evening.

Chapter III

✱ ✱ The weatherman on the radio said the snow wouldn't amount to much, but from the flurries coming down outside against the box elder tree beside the wooden sidewalk I didn't believe him. I really didn't want to believe him because it was close to Christmastime and snow was wanted by all the children and not wanted by the men—especially the ranchers, as Pa was quick to remind us time and time again. We had come into Fort Pierre for Sunday dinner, and now we sat, waiting to see if the snow was going to continue or quit.

It hadn't been a good trip so far. Mom had been in one of her holier-than-thou moods (at least, that's what Pa was able to call it; I was supposed to know enough to keep my mouth shut, but I had decided enough was enough and made mention of Pa's disdainful remark about Mom's Methodist churchgoing) and now I was hooked, with Mom livid when I told her I didn't want to go to Sunday school, much less church afterward, and had decided that I was going to join Pa and Grandpa in their heathen ways, hunting and fishing. Bad mistake that. Mom lit into me, reminding me that I had just gotten my birthday presents only the day before because I had sassed when I should have remained quiet. I had gotten the Marlin lever-action .22-caliber rifle and that had assured me, I believe, that I had crossed over into adulthood. And when she paused to catch her breath, Grandma lit into me, punctuating her phrases with quotes from old Billy Sunday sermons about the duty of a young girl and wasn't it about time I gave up trying to be a boy and started to learn how to be a lady. That's why she had given me that blue gingham dress with the little lace collar for my birthday and planned on buying me shoes to match it as soon as she could get me cornered and down to the shoe store.

Grandma took me to every Chautauqua that came through to hear the stump preachers rant and rave, steely-eyed and determined that I wouldn't follow in the footsteps of certain ne'er-do-wells like Three-fingered Louie, who ran trotlines in the summer and lazed on welfare during the winter or Ruby Ann down at the diner who painted her face so thickly that it cracked like old barnwood when she smiled. She liked to lean her big breasts on her arms that she folded over the counter in front of a man to give him a gander and a thought.

I remember once when Old Sven hobbled down the aisle to be saved, and the preacher laid his hands on him and yelled, "Heal! Heal!" and cast out the evil spirits that were keeping Old Sven from galloping down the street and into the Hop Scotch for his nightly bottle and out to the cottonwoods for a trip with the squaws in the backseat of some old junker. Old Sven had shouted, "Hallelujah!" and thrown away his cane and fallen flat on his ass when he tried to turn around.

Grandma always gave me a dime to put in the offering plate whenever one came around (almost like clockwork), a hard thing for me to do, as it always seemed to be time to pay the Lord when a new *Kid Colt* comic book showed up at the Rexall Drug Store. And, Grandma squeaked constantly while shaking her finger at me, I should behave especially good around this time of year, before Christmas, when old

Father Christmas was certainly padding around, trying to catch the young ladies in some last miscreant act in order to deny them their goodness wages on Christmas Day. I looked at Pa, but I could tell from the stony stare of his gray eyes that I had pushed things past that point where I should have pushed, and I could tell by the tightness around his lips that I had compromised as well that last bastion of maleness, for Mom turned to him, fixing him with her level stare that brooked no nonsense from man or beast, and allowed as to how it was time that he put on a tie and come with them to begin the family routine that led down the road to Christmas Eve services and fulfilled his religious obligations for the season. When Grandpa chuckled at the look of consternation on Pa's face, Grandma got into the act and allowed as to how it wouldn't hurt him none to pull his blue wool suit out of the mothballs and don his white shirt and tie and gold cuff links and come along, either.

So I got a double glare from both men as they went off to their bedrooms to dress for church, and the silence in Grandpa's green Chevrolet was so thick you could cut it with a butter knife as we drove the four blocks to church. Afterward, I got another talking-to by Mom, who just wouldn't let a thing like that die, about the obligations a person had always but more especially at this time of year. I had learned my lesson, however, and "yes, ma'amed" and "no ma'amed" my way out of it.

And then the snow came and saved me from more haranguing, falling thick and heavy, covering the back way past the elm tree down to the Old Plunge in a half hour. Mom and Pa debated well into late afternoon as to whether or not they should start back for the ranch. It was kinda tricky trying to gauge whether one should head out along the highway or not, because one never knew for certain if the snow crews had been out or how far out they had gone before thinking they were fighting a losing battle with the drifts and turning back. Then again, even that was no assurance, because sometimes the snow leaped down from Canada so fast that the snow crews couldn't keep the highways clean. Pa and Mom were reluctant to start back to the ranch until they knew for sure. In South Dakota, people held a healthy respect for the winter and kept a weather-wise eye on the day.

But now, well, we really weren't ready for this one, as the fluke storm blew up rapidly, sweeping down the open plains and between the bluffs of the Missouri River. And so we waited until finally Pa decided that it would be best if we stayed the night and took off in the morning. He put in a call to Oly Johnson and told him about our predicament, and Oly allowed as to how he thought Pa had made the right decision and he would ride over to our place and tell Stocker so he would know to do all the chores and care for the stock until we got back.

When morning came, however, things had gotten worse, and when Pa called Oly, Oly told him that the roads were blocked and he would call Pa when the snow crews had gone down the roads. But it looked like it would be at least another day or two because of the drifting. Pa asked him to go over to the Stone place and see if Johnny's father would let Johnny give Stocker a hand until we got back.

So now we waited and I rested my chin on the back of an overstuffed easy chair and gloomily watched, wishing that I could be outside. But Mom had forbidden me to go outside, as they wanted to be ready to start back home when the weather broke. Beside me lay the pile of comic books that I kept at Grandpa's house, each one having been read at least a dozen times or so in the past when I had been kept there. I remembered my birthday presents that Mom had finally let me have after a week's penance, but they did me little good now, most of them—including the lever-action rifle from Pa—remaining back at the ranch since this was supposed to have been a one-day visit. I thought briefly about going upstairs for the book from my aunt and uncle that had been among the presents—*Nevada* by Zane Grey. I liked the picture on the dust jacket: a cowboy on a spirited horse, turning and firing at a group of cowboys on lathered horses chasing him—but I finally decided I didn't feel like going up to my room.

I sighed and looked back at the snow falling. School had already been canceled for tomorrow due to this sudden blizzard that struck Fort Pierre, and although I had met the news of the school closing with enthusiasm, knowing that school also would be closed in Ithaca and I wouldn't have any make-up work to do, by now the prospect of further delay inside the house made the time drag and a full day in the house pall. I turned my head and looked at the Christmas tree and the bubble lights. Garland swags, made from pine boughs and baling wire, looped from one side of the room to the other, their apex anchored by large red cellophane paper bells that folded around back on themselves and were hooked by a small gold clip.

I sighed and slumped back into the chair and listlessly picked up another comic book, glancing at its cover: Gene Autry and his horse, Champion; Smiley Burnette standing behind Gene. I opened it and began to read, scanning the words, anticipating the plot. Over in the corner, Grandpa rustled the newspaper and rocked, the chair creaking on the backswing. Faint smells of baking brownies and fudge crept down the hallway from the kitchen. A gust of wind rattled the shutter. The blower on the coal furnace kicked on, sending a blast of hot air up through the floor grating. The room seemed stifling—hot and airless—and the light began to fade outside, turning lead gray. I sighed again and climbed out of the chair and walked down the hallway to the kitchen pantry to get a popcorn ball. I carefully selected the roundest one and began to eat. My fingers and face soon became covered with sticky syrup. The kitchen door opened and a gust of cold air rushed in.

"Well, is everybody ready?" Pa asked, bundled against the cold in his huge coat with the fur collar. His cowboy hat had been pulled down low over his ears. He stamped the snow from his boots. I looked over at Mom busily chopping carrots for a stew she and Grandma were setting. She smiled and nodded at me, the tiny tired lines around her eyes lifting a little.

"We decided to finish up some shopping while we wait to go back home. We're going over to Pierre. Would you like to come?"

"Yes, ma'am," I said firmly, and ran for the bathroom to scrub the stickiness from my fingers with the gray pumice soap Grandpa still used out of the habit he had established when he came home from working with his section gang on the railroad. I dried my hands on my shirt as I sprinted to the hall closet, where my parka hung by its hood from a wooden peg. I pulled it on and zipped it tightly against my throat, buttoning the muffler across my neck. Then I bent and pulled my overboots on, stuffing the cuffs of my pants into the boots, and buckled them tightly. I dashed to the back door and fidgeted impatiently, as Mom and Grandma carefully combed their hair and properly fixed their faces while debating whether to wear their ankle-length church coats or their knee-length working coats and tried to decide which scarf best complemented which coat. I wanted to shout that it made damn little difference which ones they picked, but I remembered the time from yesterday when I had tried to step into adulthood in one leap and kept silent.

Finally, we were ready and I opened the back door and stepped outside, leaning against the wind. Tall brown sticks that once were green hollyhock stems rasped together like cricket legs, and the brown blanket of grapevines twined thickly through chicken wire along the gallery that stretched the length of the house and billowed in and out with each gust of wind. Pa had used the large scoop shovel Grandpa kept to scoop coal into the hopper downstairs to clear a path across the fifty-foot wasteland to the garage, but the whipping snow was already threatening to fill in the path. Mom frowned and wondered aloud if this was a good idea, but Pa said that he reckoned we could be over and back before it got much worse and, even if it did, he had put the scoop shovel in the trunk of the car for good measure. Reluctantly Mom agreed, and we stepped into the car. We drove through the swirling clouds of snow on our way downtown. I sat between Pa and Grandpa in the front seat, looking at the decorations strung above the streets. The shop owners had painted their windows with pictures of winter wonderlands, and reindeer and bright red foil bells dangled over Christmas specials. I looked eagerly for the Bootery window, for I knew Santa Claus would be perched on a tiny stool, directing his elves in the making of electric trains and dolls, and the bakery window where Mama Claus took countless gingerbread men from her oven.

Pa swung to make a wide left turn like he was taking a thirty-foot dump rake through a fence gate to avoid a large manmade drift of snow in the center of the street. At the far end, where the street dead-ended into a small park at the junction of the Bad and Missouri Rivers, I saw the first strand of twisted evergreen branches arching over the street and the round face of Santa Claus winking and swinging high overhead between flakes of snow.

The trip over the Missouri River to Pierre seemed to take forever, as Pa was forced to drive slowly as the wind blew snow across the road, momentarily blinding the motorists. Pa debated a minute about going over the steel-girded bridge but at last attempted it. We were alone on the bridge, and when we dropped down on the other side, Pa breathed a silent sigh of relief.

We crept carefully down the street and Pa parked the car against the curb. The wind had begun to die down, but snow still fell in huge, soft flakes. I tried vainly to catch one with my tongue as Grandma and Mom decided to go to J. C. Penney's clothing store and then to the sewing center. Pa and Grandpa decided to visit Montgomery Ward's hardware store. I elected to follow the men, for the Ben Franklin dime store was only a few doors away from the hardware store and I could step into it while Pa and Grandpa did their shopping for Mom and Grandma.

I think this is the Christmas when Mom was supposed to get a new set of dishes, but I cannot be sure. It really doesn't matter, for Mom always received something for the house from the houseware department in the hardware store. In the meantime, I wandered the narrow aisles of the dime store, mesmerized by the toys that had been only pictures in the fall catalogs.

In the back of the store the comic books were displayed in large black wire racks. I skimmed through various issues of *Donald Duck* and *Mickey Mouse* and *Roy Rogers* and *Gene Autry* and *Rex Allen* and a rare copy of *Tom Mix*. Suddenly, a grown-up voice from above gently reminded me that the comic books were for buying and not reading, and I guiltily placed *Tom Mix* back into the rack, carefully slipping it behind one of the girls' comic books—*Archie*, I think, or maybe it was *Little Lulu*—hoping I could talk Pa out of a dime so I could buy *Tom Mix* before we returned home.

I walked back to the hardware store, searching for Pa and Grandpa, but they were not in the aisles by the fishing rods, nor by the automotive products. I took a deep breath and entered the forbidden aisle of plates and dinnerware, carefully keeping to the middle of the aisle for fear of knocking fragile china to the wooden floor. Thankfully, they weren't there, and I ducked into the small toy section but found only my friends, Eddie Thomas and Fatty Bigley, furtively playing with the model train setup despite the DO NOT TOUCH sign prominently displayed by the control board. I slipped away without them seeing me and headed to the front door. I had a pretty good idea now where Pa and Grandpa would be. I stepped back out onto the sidewalk and around the teenager sourly scraping the slushy snow from the sidewalk with a snow shovel and turned left and walked past the Goodrich tire store to the corner. I crossed the street when the light flashed green and slipped into the darkness of the Lariat Bar. They were sitting in the corner booth, drinking Tom and Jerrys. A bottle of Coca-Cola waited for me. The cherries from their Tom and Jerrys had been placed in a shot glass for me. I dropped them into the glass before adding my Coca-Cola. I leaned back against the hard wooden back of the booth and sipped my drink.

"Well, what did you find?" Pa asked. His eyes twinkled from the Tom and Jerrys, and I told him about the *Tom Mix* comic book, hinting strongly that I sure could use a dime. But he shook his head and mumbled some nonsense about Christmas being too close and would Grandpa like another Tom and Jerry before the womenfolk found them? Grandpa nodded and pulled a red tin of Eagle Claw tobacco from his overcoat pocket. He began to roll another cigarette as Pa slid from the booth and crossed to the bar with their empty glasses. I sipped from my glass and tried not to think how long it would be before somebody discovered the rare *Tom Mix* comic book. I smelled the sulfur from Grandpa's kitchen match and felt his hard forefinger poking me in the ribs. He pushed a small coin into my hand. I looked up at his large tanned, square face with the bushy steel-gray eyebrows. The right eye closed in a solemn wink, and I smiled my thanks and gulped my drink and hurried back to the dime store to claim *Tom Mix*.

I bumped into Tubby Watson as he came into the bar, and he snarled and gave me a shove. I staggered back into the room, coming up against a booth. His right eye was still closed from where Abel had punched him, and a thick scab hung like a chunk of snuff from his lip.

"Keep the hell away from here," he snarled. A cloud of bourbon fumes wafted over me. I backed away from him as he took a couple of steps toward me, raising his hand.

"Leave the girl alone," Pa said softly, a hard edge threatening beneath his words. I looked back over my shoulder. Pa stood flat-footed, his hands hanging down by his side. Grandpa slid from the booth and moved to Pa's left. Talk in the bar trailed off.

"What the hell you got this brat in here for anyway?" Tubby snarled. "This is for men, ain't it?"

"Yep," Grandpa said. "Sure is. So I reckon maybe you'd better turn around and go back out."

"I don't need—"

"Button it, Watson, or leave," Frank, the bartender, said quietly. "We don't need your attitude in here."

Watson glared at me, then turned and stumbled outside. I looked at Pa. He smiled faintly and shrugged, then turned back to the bar and ordered his drinks. Grandpa nodded at me, and I turned, leaving for the dime store to claim *Tom Mix*. I stepped outside and took a cautious look down the street. Watson stumbled into the Spur, and I hurried down the street to the Ben Franklin store.

At the comic book rack, I found Eddie and Fatty skimming the newest *Tex Ritter* western. I crept behind them and lowered my voice as deep as I could.

"Hey, didn't I tell you kids those were for buying, not reading?"

They jumped and tried to stuff the comic books back into the rack.

Fatty turned and recognized me. "Aw!" he complained. "What'd jah have to do that for?"

"Good going. I might have ripped it, and then you'd be sorry," Eddie whined.

"Scared yuh, huh?" I smirked at them. "What are you guys doing downtown?"

"Nothing," Eddie said. "Our parents are out Christmas shopping and told us to get lost."

"So you came here?" I looked around the store, standing on tiptoe to try and see through the glass of the tall counters. "I haven't seen them."

"Yeah," Eddie said disgustedly. "I guess that shows what kind of Christmas is ahead of us. Last I saw them, they were heading for J. C. Penney's. How about you?"

"Same thing," I said. Casually I reached behind the *Archie* comics and removed *Tom Mix*. "Just came in to pick this up."

Their eyes widened with envy and Eddie reached for it, but I held it behind my back.

"Lemme see it," he demanded.

"Huh-uh," I returned. I smiled triumphantly at him. "Find your own."

"You stuck that behind those *Archies*, didn't you?" Fatty accused.

"Yep."

"I'll remember that," Eddie said. He punched me on the arm. "One for the road."

I smiled and punched him back. "I'll let you read it when I get done."

"First dibs?"

I nodded.

"Second dibs?" Fatty asked hopefully.

I looked at him scornfully. "No such things as second dibs." His face fell and I relented. "But you can read it after I reread it after Eddie gets done. That'll sort of make it first dibs again."

"Gee, but you're a pal. For a girl," he said, and punched me on the shoulder. "One for the road."

I nodded and punched him back, carefully pulling it so it turned into more of a push. Fatty bawled if someone hit him too hard. I waved and headed for the cashier. The silver-haired lady at the cash register smiled merrily and brightly wished me a Merry Christmas as I hurried for the door.

When I returned to the Lariat, Pa pretended to be angry about Grandpa giving me the dime, but I could tell he really wasn't, as he had saved the maraschino cherries from their drinks for me.

"You're spoiling her," Pa said to Grandpa.

"My privilege," Grandpa said. "That's what grandpas are for."

"Well, what are fathers for?"

"To tell grandpas they're spoiling the children."

"This is great wisdom," Pa said solemnly. He raised his glass. "Do we have time for another?"

"I don't think so," Grandpa said, and nodded toward the front. I didn't have to turn around to know Mom and Grandma were threading their way through the tables to the back booth where we sat. Quickly Grandpa finished his drink and we slid from the booth.

"Are you ready?" Grandma sniffed, and tried to fix Grandpa with an iron stare, but the corners of her thin lips quivered. "Well? You should be ashamed of yourselves for dragging a young girl into a place like this."

"But I like it here," I wanted to say. And I'm not a child. I knew, however, that I would create nothing but trouble for Pa and Grandpa if I mentioned how fine it was in that dark, masculine retreat with its rich heady smells of beer and eggnog heavy with spices, let alone told them about Tubby Watson. No, better by far to keep quiet. After Sunday I was taking no chances of sassing back this close to Christmas. And as for Tubby Watson, well, that little episode belonged to Pa, and he could tell Mom when and if he wanted. Besides, he would be the one chewed out for letting me come into the place in the first place if she knew about Watson and his threat.

"Ready," Pa said.

"Not quite," Grandpa said. He turned and picked up a cardboard box from behind the booth, steadying it in his broad hands. The unmistakable clink of glass came from the box, and Grandma frowned but didn't say anything as she turned and led us out from the bar. The snow was falling a little heavier. Huge flakes falling like fat marshmallows. We made our way carefully down the street to where Pa had parked the car. Across the street, Tubby staggered out of the bar, saw us, and raised his fist, clapping his hand across his bicep. Pa made a harsh sound in his throat and started across the street, but Mom pulled him up short.

"Let it go, Tom," she said quietly. "He isn't worth the trouble."

"Someone's going to have to teach him a lesson," Pa grumbled.

"From the looks of him, I think Abel already did," Mom said. "Besides, you're just looking for a reason to fight him." A frown pulled her lips down. "That's the drink talking." She patted her auburn hair, thick as a horse's mane, the same color as mine. We even shared the spattering of freckles across our noses. In the summer her skin burnt brown, yet there was a strange translucence beneath it. The only difference between us were our eyes. Hers were green—mine blue that turned silver-gray when I became angry, or so I'm told. All the other McCaslins had dark hair and black eyes.

"All right," Pa said grudgingly. He opened the door and stood aside so we could slide in. "But he's gonna cause more trouble somehow. Mark my words."

And I remembered Abel's words as we stood there in the dark outside the dance hall.

"That's a bad man," he'd said frowning.

I glanced at him curiously. "How can you tell?"

"I can smell the bad on him," he said quietly.

"Smell the bad?"

"Yep. Like smelling your armpit after working all afternoon on a hot summer day just after it's rained and the air is thick and hard to breathe. You know? Like overripe turnips freshly dug."

And I remembered Watson's sour stench from the bar, and a vague misgiving came over me as Pa pulled carefully away from the curb and we began our slow crawl down the street and back over the bridge to Grandpa's house in Fort Pierre. In the dark, I saw Watson's face, his eyes the color of stagnant water and the crooked tooth in front that snaggled over the one next to it, brown-stained from the nickel's worth of tobacco that he chewed until the suption had all slipped from it, and the dark stubble of his beard that covered his cheeks and jowls.

And I was afraid.

Chapter IV

Spotty shied nervously away from a tuft of grama grass poking up through a spare snow skiff when the gust of wind hit it. I pressed my knees against his side and ran my hand down his mane, patting his neck, soothing him. Pa glanced over at me and gestured irritably to bring up the drag as we moved the north herd down toward the home pasture. Abel moved his dun along the west flank while Pa held down the east. Stocker worked as a swing rider, anchoring the herd against the north fence and sweeping south. We had been lucky; a rare chinook came down hard on the heels of the blizzard, melting the snow and giving us a chance to bring the last of our herd down to the pasture south of the house for holding during the winter. Pa had felt the chinook coming the night before and called Abel, who rode up across country from his place on Plum Creek to help us with the cattle. Some ranchers scoffed at Pa for claiming that he could feel a chinook coming down, but I had never known him to be wrong. And I never knew how he knew.

I stood in the stirrups and pulled my horse around to the rear, slipping down a small draw to bring up an old heifer and her fall calf.

"Get up there, damn you! It's for your own good," I said. Cattle have to be among the dumbest of God's creatures, I thought, leaning back against the cantle as my horse scrambled up the draw bank after the heifer and her calf. I caught a movement out of the corner of my eye and glanced down toward the plum thicket at the end of the draw and saw a coyote fading back into the naked branches. My hand dropped automatically toward the rope tied beside the saddle horn, then reluctantly came away. I had heard the old cowboys in Fort Pierre tell how Wally Bates had hunted coyotes with a rope, the only one who had success-fully managed to catch one with a noose. But there was no way I could swing a noose in that thicket, and besides, I had no desire to face Pa's anger if he caught me away from the drag. For a moment I wished that I had strapped my new Marlin on the saddle, but there had been no time for that. We had no way of knowing how long the chinook would last or if there was another blizzard behind it. When the weather turned like it had, no rancher wasted a single minute of it.

It took us eight hours to bring the herd into the pasture, and I knew something was wrong as soon as we rode into the home yard and Mom came to the door and stepped out across the threshold. The wind blew her dress hard against her legs and she held it tightly to her thighs with one hand while she pressed against her stomach with the other. Her face was tight, lines deeply etched. She looked a little gray.

"Abel!" she shouted, and gestured.

Abel's head swung over, his face drawing down as he rode over to Mom. I started to follow, but Pa pushed his big roan between us and looked at me, shaking his head.

"You've got cattle to move down to the stock tank," he said lowly.

I started to argue, but one look at his face told me that this wasn't the time to sass back. Obediently I turned the horse's head and began riding slowly behind the cattle. Pa lifted the roan into a trot and rode over to where Mom was talking urgently with Abel. Then I saw Abel wheel his horse and ride away, the dun coming up into a lope as he rode through the gate. The last of the cattle began walking down the slope toward the stock tank, and I rode back through the fence, pausing to latch the gate behind me. Pa had stepped down from the roan and held the reins in his hand, his other arm around Mom as they watched Abel disappear over a rise.

"What's wrong?" I asked.

Mom turned away from me, but not before I caught a hint of tears in her eyes. She walked back inside the house without speaking, both hands pressing against her stomach. She closed the door behind her.

"Let's get these horses put up," Pa said roughly. He raised his head and looked at the sky. "Never can tell. There might be a change coming and we'll need 'em then to keep the cattle from going down."

I knew his worry; a cow would not lick the mucus from its nostrils, and if the mucus froze or if snow clogged its nostrils, it would suffocate. If a blizzard came and lasted a long time, then we would have to ride around the herd, pulling the cows up by their tails and unclogging their nostrils so they could breathe.

"Abel," I began, but Pa shook his head and stepped back into his stirrup, swinging up into his saddle. He rode down to the barn. I took one last look up at the now empty rise and followed him, curiosity eating at me, along with a dread.

Dinner had been subdued, with Mom and Pa making small talk, pointedly keeping from mentioning anything about Abel except to say that his family had some trouble. The telephone rang halfway through dinner. Pa paused, looked at Mom, then rose and walked over to the telephone on the wall by the door. Mom gathered the plates and took them to the sink and laid out small plates and clean forks. She put an apple pie next to her place and quickly sliced it, laying a thin slice of cheddar cheese on each piece. Pa returned to the table as she finished. He sat, cut the tip off his piece, chewed it, nodded.

"Good," he said. He cut another piece and lifted it on his fork, pausing. He looked significantly at Mom. "Abel hasn't made it home, yet."

Mom frowned. "He cut across country. He should've been there by now, shouldn't he? How far is it?"

Pa shook his head. "Mrs. Six Feathers said she was gonna stay in Pierre at the hospital. If he calls here, we're to give him the message."

Mom looked at Pa but didn't say anything. Her lips tightened and she rose, taking my plate and hers, and crossed to the sink. I could tell by the set of her shoulders that something was bothering her, but Pa didn't say anything, just finished his pie, chewing each bite slowly and methodically, occasionally washing his mouth with a swallow of coffee. I waited for him to say something, but he stared off into the distance, lost in his own thoughts. He scraped his fork across his plate, then rose, picked it up from the table, and looked at me.

"Best go up to bed, now," he said.

"It's early," I protested automatically. "I thought I'd listen to *Inner Sanctum* tonight on the radio. Ain't no school tomorrow," I added hopefully. I had been waiting for this Christmas vacation for a long time and so far I hadn't seen much of my plans. The way things were going I'd be back in that six-room, asphalt-side-shingled schoolhouse without having done much but move cattle. And then it was a long time until Easter without a break from Miss Sexton—one of those ravaged middle-aged women with wattles and iron-gray hair pulled back so tightly in a bun that it screeched. She had long narrow feet like rails and was so skinny I'd swear she had to hop around in the shower to get wet. And she was over-handy with a willow switch on the smaller ones who had a hard time learning. She no longer tried switching the older ones after Billy Anderson quietly took it away from her and broke it in half when she struck him over the shoulders. He politely handed it back to her in a gesture that made him a legend in the school. I had her scheduled for the next term, and I wasn't looking forward to the experience. I also knew there'd be some resentment there as the school had decided to jump me a grade and I was going to be the youngest one in the class.

"Isn't," Mom corrected. She turned pale suddenly and gasped and turned back to the sink, holding her stomach, her shoulders arched high like a buzzard as she curved over the sink.

"Mom," I said, alarmed, and took a step toward her, but Pa dropped a rough hand on my shoulder, holding me. I looked up at him.

Pa threw a quick glance at her back, then said, "All right.

But after that, bed. I want to ride the south fence tomorrow and you can come along. We might pick up a stray or two down in one of the draws."

"Tomorrow is Sunday," Mom said tightly, but Pa shook his head and I could tell from the set of his shoulders that talk was closed on the subject. He could be stubborn as an old mule when he had made a decision.

"I'm sure the good Lord will understand if we take care of our herd," Pa said dryly. "Just as I'm certain that Christ took care of his flock on Sunday as well."

Mom took a deep, shaky breath and straightened. Her face was pale and she brushed a strand of hair back off her forehead. She started to argue, but Pa cut her off, saying, "Enough. Sam's working with me on the morrow, now."

I started to argue, but he turned away and carried his plate to the sink. I knew my day was planned for me and sighed and rose, walking into the living room. I crossed to the radio and turned it on, adjusting the dial to try and get rid of the static, finally settling on what sounded the best. I pulled up my favorite seat, a red-and-white footstool that had been my horse when I was younger, and listened to *The Lone Ranger*. I sprawled over the footstool on my belly, stretched out toward the radio. Mom came in and took her chair under the floor lamp while Pa crossed to his rocker, sat, and put on his glasses as he reached for a copy of *The Stockman*. Mom opened her sewing basket at the foot of her chair. She picked up one of Pa's work shirts and began sewing a button back on it. It seemed like he was always losing his buttons. Must be a man thing.

The wind picked up and whistled around the eaves. A dry rattle came against the window. I looked up at Pa; he had lifted his head, listening. He sensed my stare and looked at me and slowly nodded. A board creaked. A cold breeze came from somewhere and then the furnace coughed and a blast of hot air came from the furnace grate behind me. A vague uneasiness moved over me. I shivered and started to sit up, and then I heard the sound of a door creaking open on the radio and I moved closer to the radio. I sighed.

Chapter V

Pa was right; when I awoke in the morning and cleaned a small circle through the frosted narrow clerestory window in the dormer of my room to peer out, I saw nothing but a field of white. Down at the corral, the horses moved listlessly through the drifts and on the hill. I felt the cold seeping already through my flesh to my bones and wished that for once I was going to church with Mom instead of sitting on the cold leather of my saddle and riding my paint through the drifts. I would be nigh onto frozen by the time we returned, and we wouldn't return until dark. Mom would have done my chores by then except for putting up my horse, which Pa's iron rule kept anyone from doing but the rider. But then I recalled what had happened the previous Sunday at church when the good Reverend John T. Boskins got to yammering on about suffering the little children to come unto him and I was yawning and fighting to stay awake in the heavy heat of the little brownstone church. Somewhere around the time when he got to bringing in the sheaves and feeding the fishes or some such thing (I never could get the hang of his convoluting ways of talking), I nodded off, and my snores caused quite a titter and tither among the congregation before Mom, red-faced with embarrassment, managed to nudge me awake with an elbow jab to my ribs that nigh broke every one. Later, when we were on our way home in the Oldsmobile, she lit into me.

"It's time you started growing up, Samantha," she said, keeping her eyes fixed firmly on the road. "You can't pretend to be something you're not."

"I'm not pretending," I protested.

"Look at how you're dressed," she said.

I glanced down at my new jeans and shirt and jacket. My boots were polished and I knew my hair was combed—although that wasn't much as it was short enough that I only had to run a comb once or twice through it to get it to lay straight.

"What's wrong with the way I look?" I asked defensively.

"You're not a boy," she said. "And it's time you started learning that. There's a whole difference between boys and girls."

"Just because I'm a girl doesn't mean I can't dress like this," I said.

"It isn't just about the way you dress," she said a touch angrily.

That stumped me and I opened my mouth to say so, but wisely decided that discretion was called for at this point in the conversation.

"If you're not careful, you're going to become a heathen like that no-account Huck Finn Mark Twain wrote about."

I caught myself just in time from "yes, ma'aming" her and wondered if maybe Johnny Stone might be willing to go in with me in building a raft and floating down Bad River to the muddy Missouri and on down the line to the Mississippi and on down that to New Orleans. Heck, I thought as we drove on home in blessed silence, we might even be able to make the raft such that we could go right on down to South America and visit those beaches of Venezuela where all those girls and men hung around in Band-Aid bathing suits, according to the *National Geographic* magazine I had discovered in the pile in the attic and now kept under a pile of comic books tucked in the back of my closet.

We drove over the Bad River and I looked down at the waters rolling in roiling rings—thick, gray, and ominous—down away from us and thought about the danger, remembering when they pulled Donny Peterson out of the river and tried to revive him with a pull motor and failed, and thought that maybe we had better wait until the spring runoff had settled. But I still made a mental note to bring the subject up with Johnny at our next meeting, as long as we were out of earshot of the adults who always put a kibosh on our plans.

I rose and shivered my way into my clothes, then picked up my boots and hurried on stockinged toes down the stairs into the kitchen, where Mom was busily turning bacon and eggs and pouring fresh batter into the cast-iron skillet on the stove. I set my boots next to the stove to warm them and grabbed a glass of orange juice.

"Sip," Mom warned as I started to gulp it down. I obeyed and sipped as long as her gray eyes were on the glass level, then drained it when she turned back to flipping the bacon.

"Can I have coffee this morning since I'm riding out with Pa?" I asked.

"No," she answered. She wiped her hands on the dish towel she had tucked into the top of her calico apron. "You're too young. But I've made hot chocolate for you. It's in the pan."

I made a face behind her back, but I took the hot chocolate anyway 'cause I knew that I would be cold as an ice cube in half an hour as we made our way down toward the south fence line. She handed a plate heaped high with eggs and bacon and pancakes and nodded at the table where she had already set out the syrup and the jelly she had made from the chokecherries I had gathered in the spring. I sat down in my place and layered the pancakes with the jam and poured a hefty dollop of syrup over the top of them and began packing it in.

I heard the back door open and slam shut, then Pa's boots echo across the wood floor of the porch as he came into the mudroom. He opened the door and entered, bringing the smell of the cold with him. He nodded at me and limped up to his place at the table and eased into the chair, grimacing as his stiff muscles loosened. Sometimes when it was cold or he overworked, Pa's foot took to bothering him. A steer had stomped on his foot, breaking it, but Pa hadn't paid much attention to it and by the time he got to a doctor, the doctor said he would have to rebreak it before he could set it. But Pa hadn't had the time for that then, and that had been six years before. Now he figured he might as well put up with it.

Mom put a plate to match mine in front of him and handed him a cup of coffee. He spilled a bit into the saucer and blew on it to cool it, then drank it on down and said, "It's cold out; better make sure you got on your long johns."

"Already have," I said around a mouthful of bacon.

"And wear your chaps," he said. "They'll break the wind on your legs. And your hooded sweatshirt. Ain't gonna take a chance on getting frostbit."

"If it's that cold maybe you'd better stay at home," Mom said. She looked at me. "And we can forget about church, too. Although it might do someone a bit of good if she rode her horse to that church."

"Don't think they'll be holding church," Pa said, cutting slowly into his stack of pancakes. "The maintainer ain't cleared the road yet. Nobody ain't going nowhere in a car. 'Course I expect the Andersons will probably hook up their Clydesdales to that sleigh of theirs and take it on into Ithaca to church, but Oly never did have the good sense that God gave a grasshopper."

"And you do, riding out in this to check the fence?" she asked dryly.

"Have to make sure the wire's still up. Cattle prices are going up after the first of the year, and one lost is money out of our pockets. 'Sides, it's a part of our obligation. I've already sent Stocker out along the north." He nodded at me. "We'll take the south."

And that took care of Mom's argument. Pa was real big on what he called obligation. I never could put my finger on exactly what he meant by that, and one day when I asked Mom she said it was a deal you made with God to take care of His creatures when you decided to be a rancher. Pa smiled and said that was as good an explanation as any he could offer, although it wasn't exactly right, and when I asked him what was exactly right, he said that I would find out someday when I had growed enough. And when I asked when that would be, he had shrugged and said I'd know it when the time came and went on about his business. I reckoned this was one of those times that I would understand about when I got older, although right now I wasn't feeling like I wanted to under-stand it at all and just wanted to curl up in the living room in front of the fire with a book and read the day away.

By ten o'clock it had begun to snow again and we were working our way up along the draw that led down to Plum Creek. The day had been worse than I had imagined. Twice we had to pull an old heifer out of a drift and send her ambling back across the prairie where we would be able to find her when we turned back for home. We found the old brindled steer mired down, too, and that took a lot of work on the part of both of us to drag him out, as he kept fighting the rope. I had a rope burn across my thigh that I knew would send me swearing when I stepped into a hot bath at the end of the day, and I was cold, my feet numb in two pairs of socks and my boots and my fingers near lumps in my lined gloves. I didn't bother thinking about my face but was thankful that I had grabbed a scarf on my way out the door and wrapped it around my head, leaving just enough room for my eyes so I looked like a bandit set to rob the First National Bank.

I watched a coyote fold down a gully to the purple shadows and into a chokecherry thicket, a gray shadow against the mud and snow. I glanced up at Pa.

"I saw him," he said, and turned Fritz, his roan, up the gully, following the tracks. A coyote wouldn't be out in this weather unless he had found some food, and chances were that we would find the remains of a heifer he had pulled down or a calf somewhere up his back trail. I turned Spotty and trailed Pa as we made our way out of the gully and up onto the flat leading back to the hills and Wild Horse Creek that roamed over the pasture and down to the river. We hadn't gone far when we found him, frozen stiff as a board next to the fence. The coyotes hadn't had time to get at him much and it wouldn't have mattered if they had; I recognized Abel Six Feathers as sure as if he was standing whole beside me.

"Ah," Pa said. He sat for a moment staring down at Abel's leg sticking under the wire, then climbed down stiffly and knelt beside him. "Give me a hand," he said, and I stepped down from the saddle, nearly folding as my legs took a moment to recover from the cold. I draped Spotty's reins over the wire and squatted beside Pa. We pulled Abel the rest of the way out of the snow, trying to turn him over, but his body was too stiff. Then, Pa swore and I paused, staring at him for a moment; then I looked down at Abel's back and saw where the bullet had taken him between the shoulders.

"Let go," Pa said, and we eased Abel back down in his place. Pa stood and glanced at the sky, a lead gray, the flakes falling thick and heavy and looking like they had no intention of stopping soon.

"You ride on back to the house and call the sheriff," he said. "Leave the saddle on Spotty and saddle up the sorrel gelding for Red and bring him on out here. I'll stay here with Abel."

"Pa, the snow," I began, but he smiled gently and cut me off.

"Sam, we can't leave Abel out here and we can't take him in until the sheriff gets out here and takes a look," he said.

I looked around at the barren white plain and shook my head. "Ain't nothing to see, Pa," I said.

"Go," he said firmly, and I turned and stepped back up in the saddle. I paused and watched as he tied Fritz to a creosote post and pulled his .308 Winchester from its scabbard. I touched the Marlin in its scabbard beneath my leg and reined Spotty around and put my heels to his ribs, cutting across the pasture to the other line where I would swing north and pick up the road, hoping that the maintainer had been through to clear it. I hoped Pa would be okay until I got back. If I got back. The air felt calm and still but queer as if a blue norther was backing itself up, readying for a rip-tearing roar down from Canada and across the plains. If it hit, we wouldn't be getting back to Pa until it was over and Pa wouldn't be coming home. Pa was out in the open. I rode harder.

Chapter VI

The storm held off until the three of us—Red Thomas, the Haakon County sheriff, and Pa and me—got Abel back to the house. The sheriff had ridden the sorrel in a wide loop around Abel's body after we had let the wire down for him, but found nothing. I knew he was just going through the motions anyway, as everything that hadn't been covered by snow before Abel was shot was covered over now. He stepped down off the sorrel and knelt beside Abel and shook his head.

"I sure wish you wouldn't have moved him, Mr. McCaslin," he said. "I might be able to line up something otherwise."

"We dropped him right back in the same spot," Pa answered. "If you could've lined up something before, you can do it now."

Red nodded and looked west along the line leading from Abel's feet. He nodded and pointed at the hills across the pasture. "Well, then, if I had to guess, I'd say the shot had to come from somewhere up there along that thicket line."

"Seems reasonable," Pa said dryly. "Especially since his feet are pointing in that direction. And that thicket's tucked into a fold of the hills. Good place to wait out of the wind."

Red scratched his head under his hat and blew on his fingers, warming them. "Yeah, but what I can't figure is how anyone knew he was comin' this way to go back home. That's what you said when we was riding out here, wasn't it?" he said, turning to me.

"Yes, sir," I answered. "Me and Pa and Abel had brought down the stock like I told you and Mom was waiting for him when we got back. He took off across the hills right after she spoke to him. I don't know what about," I added, looking significantly at Pa.

Pa ignored my hint and pointed to the south toward the reservation.

"It's shorter by about thirty miles that way," Pa said. "He could cut across Reynolds's pasture and cross the river down by Frenchman's Crossing instead of going up and around by way of Midland. Anyone who knew he would be going home would know he'd be going home that way. Always did."

"And who knew he'd be going that way 'sides you three?" the sheriff asked.

Pa shrugged. "Don't know. Someone who listened in on the telephone call would know, I suppose." Everyone in the country had a party line at the time. "Or"—he paused deliberately—"the one who did that to his daughter. He'd know."

"What's that?" I asked. They ignored me.

"Uh-huh," Red said, looking sorrowfully at the ground. "That's what I thought. Guess I just had to hear you say it." He looked up at the sky, then hawked and spat. "Well, reckon we've done all that we can out here. Ain't going to find nothing out here till this shit clears off."

"Can't leave him out here," Pa said. He looked over at my pony. "Bring Spotty over here and tie him off on the fence post, Sam. We'll put Abel on him and you can ride in double with me."

It wasn't as easy as Pa said, though. Abel was froze up

pretty stiff and we had to tie him across my saddle like a board, lacing his hands and feet together with a rope under Spotty's belly, who danced nervously under Abel's weight. But we finally had him packed awkwardly on Spotty's back and made our way slowly through the snow, which was falling heavier and heavier as we crossed the pasture and eased our way down through the deepening drifts along the fence below the hills, following it to the gate.

When we got to the home place, the snow had drifted the road shut and the ambulance that was supposed to have come out to meet us at the ranch had been stranded in Midland. The only thing to do with Abel was to put him in the tack room. We ran a rope around the rafters and under Abel's arms, lifting him in the air to keep the mice from him. He hung, swaying slightly, the toes of his boots a good two feet off the ground, his arms spread in macabre imitation of a man crucified. His eyes stared dully down at us, his lips frozen back from his teeth in a grimace of pain.

I swallowed, suddenly aware of death although I had been around it all my life with the cattle and hog butcherings and my baby brother dying in Midland from pneumonia in '49. But for some reason, I never made a connection with the ugliness of it until now. Not even when we had found Abel. I guess it had to do with not having time to think about it until now. Pa's big hand pressed gently on my shoulder, turning me and pushing me toward the door. I stumbled out into the white, breathing deeply of the cold air and turning my face into the wind. My eyes teared and my nose began to run. I pinched my nose and blew, leaning over so the snot wouldn't run on my coat.

"Cold," I mumbled, and shivered.

"Uh-huh," Pa said. "Goes right through a person, don't it?" He hawked and spat.

I stole a glance at him to see if he was poking fun at me, but he stood facing the wind too, tears seeping from his leathery face, trickling down through the sun creases. He shook himself, a burly bear, clapped his hands together, and turned to Red.

"How about a drink to chase off the chill?" he asked. "You'll stay the night."

It wasn't a question but a statement of fact, for only a damned fool would try to get through that blizzard. Red nodded, huddling deeper into his greatcoat. "Yeah, that would be nice." He cast a look over his shoulder at the tack door. "And . . ." He let his voice trail off significantly. I knew what he was thinking, though, and envied the men for their whiskey, which would help numb the thought of Abel hanging up like a side of beef in the tack room. Hot cocoa wouldn't nudge that thought away.

We crossed up to the house and stomped our boots clean on the stoop before going up into the porch and mudroom. Mom had the hot cocoa ready for me and pretended not to notice as Pa started to lead the sheriff into his office, where he kept his whiskey in a closet next to the filing cabinet. Mom took a dim view of Pa's nightly toddy and often made a pointed remark about whiskey being one of the devil's tools, but Pa ignored her Methodist ways. I guess tonight she was aware that to say anything would be stepping outside the boundaries of marital griping.

"Have a cup of cocoa to warm yourself, then go up and take a hot bath," she ordered. She wiped her hands on her apron and turned, leaning back against the sink. She grimaced and pressed her fingers against her stomach as if a stab of pain had struck. "You can mix me one, too," she said as the men walked across the kitchen. Pa stopped and gave her a curious look. She lifted her chin defensively and said, "It's been cold in here, too, today."

He nodded and paused to take a tray of ice cubes from the refrigerator and carry it into the office, where he dumped them into his ice bucket. Mom caught me staring at her and reddened. "You drink that cocoa now and march upstairs, you hear?" she ordered.

"Yes, Mom," I said, and quickly took a large swallow, promptly burning my tongue and lip. I carried the cup upstairs and to the bathroom; I turned the faucets on and sat on the toilet lid, sipping the cocoa while the tub filled with hot water, feeling the cold ache deep within my bones ease away as the room filled slowly with steam. And I thought about Abel out in the cold tack room, his body slowly stiffening as the temperature dropped and the snow fell thicker and thicker through the night. That night I felt Abel's spirit moving slowly in the darkness around me, and I awoke, sweating in the midnight of my soul.

Chapter VII

✦ ✦ Christmas Eve. I should have been happy, but a strange melancholy set in. The ambulance took Abel into Pierre to St. Mary's Hospital for an autopsy before releasing his body to his wife for burial back at Pine Ridge. Pa and I took a side of beef over to Abel's widow to help out until things got settled, but his wife didn't say much; she just stood there and cried while her son and daughter hid behind her calico skirts. Pa glanced down at me, then gently took her arm and led her inside their house, ordering me to stay by the pickup. Sarah, Abel's daughter, stood in the doorway and stared at me with burning eyes, black like slate. She had been beaten and her arm broke, and I could feel the hate of her stare searing me long after Pa and I climbed back in the pickup for the trip back to the ranch. When I asked Pa what had happened to her, the tiny muscles at the end of his jawline bunched angrily and his nostrils flared. He told me that it wasn't seemly to talk about another's grief, and I could tell from his tone of voice that I had better not push him on that subject. We drove along the country road in silence for a long while, until Pa cleared his throat and allowed as to how we really needed to go into Pierre to do some last-minute Christmas shopping.

I sighed and he glanced at me, his brows drawing together, and said that there were some things that one didn't need to know and he wasn't speaking about being older. I understood what he meant about it not being my business, but I didn't like it. When I'm interested enough to ask a question, I don't like to be put off with such things as "Wait until you're older" or "You don't need to know that." But I did agree with him about one person's grief is a private affair. I had heard enough of the old biddies gossiping after church to know that it's just in some people's nature to take pleasure in another person's suffering.

Mom was ready when we got home, and Pa told me to run up and change into a clean pair of jeans and my other boots while he talked with her. I hustled upstairs and down the hall to my room and dropped down beside the furnace grate that acted like a funnel for conversation. Sunlight streaked in, latticing the room with yellow slashes filled with dust motes. I caught a few words such as "taking it hard" and "rape" and "badly beaten," but I couldn't stay listening any longer and hurried into my jeans and a fresh flannel shirt. I pulled on my Sunday boots and scurried down the hall and clumped down the stairs. Pa glanced at me as I came into the living room, then grinned and clapped his hands together and rose. Mom slipped on her coat and grimaced with pain, taking a deep breath as she held onto the door frame for a second before nodding and saying that it was time we were going if we were to have any time for shopping at all.

Soon we were off in the Oldsmobile, taking the Bad River Road up through Capa and Van Metre and Wendt to Fort Pierre. Of course, no trip to Fort Pierre was complete unless Pa managed to squeeze in a little business on the side, and this was no exception. As we drove into Fort Pierre, Pa mentioned that this would also be a good time to make arrangements for a few head of cattle to be sold after the New

Year. Mom and I exchanged weary looks as Pa stopped at the stockyards and sale barn. After promising that he would only be a minute, he got out and walked into the office. I knew that he was good for a half hour or so and told Mom that I wanted to look at the stock waiting to be sold. She cautioned me not to get dirty, and I stepped out of the Oldsmobile and walked around to the side of the sale barn to look at the cattle in the holding pens.

I climbed up on the fence and stared down at the men working the cattle. Tubby Watson and another cowboy had thrown a yearling that had missed fall castration, tying his legs off with pigging strings, while the veterinarian moved down the line, his scalpel flashing in the winter light. The yearling bawled and struggled to free himself, and Tubby had to sit on the yearling's head to hold him down to the ground. The veterinarian worked quickly, removing the testicles and dropping them in a small stainless-steel bucket he carried. When he moved away from the yearling, Watson tried to loosen the tie strings, but the yearling's struggles had cinched the knot tight. He broke a fingernail, swore, and jammed his fingers into his mouth, kicking the yearling. His partner allowed that there was no call for doing that, and Tubby told him to shut up, then pulled a knife out of his pocket and opened the cutting blade, deftly snipping the tie strings and freeing the yearling. The yearling leaped to his feet, bawling with relief at finally being set free, and ran awkwardly away to the other side of the corral. But it was the knife in Watson's hand that drew my eyes, a Stockman Yellowboy like the one Abel had carried. Watson looked up and caught me staring at the knife in his hand.

"What the hell you staring at?" he demanded. Then he

swore, calling me a couple of names that hadn't made the Good Book.

"Your knife," I said, then caught myself as his eyes narrowed. His thumb moved up and snapped the blade shut, and I caught a glimpse of the black spider's web crack down the center of the handle and knew it was Abel's. He dropped the knife in his pocket and started toward the fence. I stepped down and walked away between the fences, trying to be nonchalant about the whole affair.

"Hey, kid!" he said loudly.

I glanced back; he was climbing over the corral fence. My stomach lurched and I scurried down the cow run and into the sale arena. The place was empty, cavernous, and I heard his boots thudding on the runway planks behind me.

I ran up the ramp to the door only to find it locked and barred. My heart began to hammer in my chest. I ducked down on hands and knees behind the VIP seats and began to crawl around the arena.

"I know you're in here, kid," Watson said. He laughed. "Come on! Show yourself. Ain't no way out 'cept by me and I ain't gonna move. I know that other door's locked."

I stole a glance over the top of the seats. He stood smack in the middle of the cow run. I dropped back down on my hands and knees in despair. How long would it be before Pa missed me and came to find me? Or Mom? And would they come in time? I swallowed painfully and felt my bladder threaten to burst. Tiny beads of perspiration formed on my forehead. I knew that Watson would hurt me if he found me. Even if I managed to convince him that I didn't know anything. He had that threatening aura around him that all kids recognize in an adult, something that warns the kids away from adults with a streak of cruelty to them.

My hand scraped across the cement as I started to crawl down the line. I felt a bolt that had dropped from a seat beneath my palm. An idea formed. I picked it up and glanced quickly over the top of the seats. He was staring off away from me, his eyes slowly traversing the dark on his right. I threw the bolt high in the air toward the seats across the arena. It struck and ricocheted down the concrete steps.

"Ha! Gotcha!" he crowed, and ran across the arena, stepping up into the section of seats. I waited until he was four rows up, then crept around the edge of the aisle and scurried down to the cow run. He heard my heels on the wooden planks and yelled, "Hey, you little bitch!"

But I ignored him and ran down the cow run and back outside, cutting through the vet chute and back to the parking lot. Pa was standing on the running board of a pickup parked next to our Oldsmobile, craning his neck as he looked over the lot. Annoyance flitted across his face as I ran up to him.

"Pa!" I gasped. I grabbed his hand and stepped close to him. "Pa! He's got Abel's knife!"

"What? Who?" He squatted on his heels beside me, his stern face scant inches from mine, his washed blue eyes staring hard into mine. "What are you talking about, Sam?"

I swallowed and took a deep breath. "Tubby Watson. I saw him over in the vet corral. He used Abel's knife to cut the pigging strings on a yearling they were castrating."

"You sure?" He shook me gently. "Think carefully, now. You sure it was Abel's knife? A knife's a knife and all, you know."

"Pretty sure," I said. "A Yellowboy with a crack like a

spider's web on the handle beneath the shield. I seen Abel use it plenty of times. You have, too, Pa!"

He straightened slowly, his eyes narrowing as he stared behind me. I turned my head quickly and saw Watson standing down at the end of the parking lot. He turned and walked away as Pa's hand came down on my shoulder, squeezing.

"What do you think, Tom?" Mom asked from the pickup.

"Pa," I said. I stopped to take a deep breath. "Pa, I'm certain. That was Abel's knife. He chased me up into the sale arena, too, when he saw me looking at him."

"Tom," Mom said.

"I think it makes sense," Pa said. He opened the back door and gave me a gentle push, shoving me inside. "In fact, it makes damn good sense. You remember the fight he had with Abel a few months back? Abel beat him pretty good. I wouldn't put it past Watson at all. Anyone who would use a cattle prod on a horse would do anything."

"What are you going to do?" Mom asked, twin frown lines appearing between her eyes. She glanced back at me. "Are you all right?"

I nodded. "Yeah. I gotta pee, though."

A tiny grin touched her lips. "Yes, I suppose you do," she said. She looked at Pa. "Well?" She glanced at her watch. "We've got time."

"Before what?" I asked.

"Never mind," Pa said. "We'll take care of that." He climbed into the Oldsmobile and started the engine. "I reckon we'll go on over to the sheriff's office and let him work on this thing."

"What about Watson?" Mom asked.

He shook his head. "Don't care about him. That's the sheriff's job. Ours is to tell what we know."

"He might get rid of the knife," Mom said.

Pa glanced at her, then into the rearview mirror at me. "Does he know you saw that knife?"

I nodded. "Yeah," I said miserably. "He asked what I was staring at and I said, 'Your knife.' But I didn't tell him that I recognized it," I added hopefully. "Maybe he didn't figure out that I recognized it."

"Uh-huh," Pa said dryly, and drove out of the parking lot, turning right onto the highway leading back to the Y that split around the hill separating part of Fort Pierre. He took the right-hand fork and drove on down to the courthouse and parked.

"Come on," he said roughly. He glanced at Mom. "You'd better come, too. If Watson had a hand in Abel's death and thinks Sam knows something, then I don't wanna give him a chance at you."

"Oh, Tom!" she said, and started to laugh, but a quick look at the grim set to Pa's face stopped her, and she opened the car door and quickly stepped out into the slush in the gutter.

We crossed to the door and entered, climbing the eight wooden steps up to the main corridor, then down to the sheriff's office. Jack Frost looked up from his desk as we came in, and motioned for us to go on across to his office.

"I take it you know about Abel Six Feathers," Pa said.

Frost nodded, a frown forming across his wide brow. His face was beefy and his shoulders strained the seams of his shirt. He had turned back his sleeves, and I noted the marine anchor and globe tattooed on his thick forearm.

"The Injun?" he said. "The one Red brought into St. Mary's killed down by Ithaca?"

Pa nodded. "He was killed on our land by our south fence. He was on his way home."

"Yeah, I remember," Frost said. "His daughter got raped or something like that, I recall. Sorry, ma'am," he apologized, his face reddening slightly. "That sort of slipped out." He glanced at me and did a double take. He blushed and shook his head. "I guess I wasn't thinking much."

"That happens occasionally," Mom said coolly. The sheriff's face reddened deeper until it looked like old liver.

"Yes," Pa said. "Well, we was over at the sale barn setting up for some cows to be shipped after the New Year and my daughter saw Tubby Watson with Abel's knife."

The sheriff glanced at me. "A knife's a knife," he said uncertainly. "What makes you think it was the Injun's?"

"It was his," I said defensively. "Had a dark crack like a spider's web along the handle below the shield. A Stockman Yellowboy."

"Maybe he gave it to Tubby," the sheriff said. "There's all kinda reasons possible. An' how many knives—Yellerboys—could have the same crack?"

"It was his," I insisted. " 'Sides, he had it with him the day he left." Pa glanced at me. "He cut a whang of leather to tie a new hondo on my rope before we left to bring in the cattle that day, remember, Pa?"

"I had forgotten," Pa said. "You're right. He had it that day."

"What reason would this Watson have to shoot the Injun?"

"Abel beat the hell out of him back in October," Pa said. "And his name is Abel, not Injun, Sheriff."

"Sorry. Bad habit." Frost blushed again and leaned back in his chair, frowning at the ceiling for a long moment. He shook his head. "Well, it's flimsy, but"—he rose and took his hat off the window ledge behind him—"it bears looking into. And we've hanged people on less. Could be a thousand and one reasons for that knife to be there or one similar. But let's see what Watson has to say about his whereabouts on that day."

"And he chased me through the sale barn when I saw it," I said. Pa gave me a strange look.

The sheriff paused, giving me a strange look, too. "Now why would he do a thing like that?"

"Unless he knew Sam had seen something," Pa said. "And if it turns out to be nothing, I want an accounting as to why he treated my daughter the way he did. She caught him beating on Abel and came and got me and some of the fellows to break it up," he added to the sheriff's look. " 'Sides, I caught Watson mistreating stock back in April or May, thereabouts, and fired him on the spot. He had tied a horse off against the corral after the horse slipped him and was using a cattle prod on it." He nodded at me. "Sam caught him with that, too."

The sheriff nodded. "Maybe you'd better tell me the whole story from beginning to end. Beginning with you," he said, nodding at me.

And so I told the whole story as we all climbed into the sheriff's car and drove back down to the sale barn. Pa's face got darker and darker as I explained how Watson had chased me into the sale arena and how I had slipped away from him. The sheriff kept looking at Pa, and when I finished, he cleared his throat.

"Now, I appreciate what you're thinking, Mr. McCaslin, but it would be better all around if you'd let me handle it," he said. Pa looked at him steadily. "I mean that, now. Just let me handle it."

"All right," Pa said softly. "For now. But I intend on having a little talk with him later."

"Mr. McCaslin—" the sheriff began.

"Tom," Mom said.

They stopped and glanced at each other. Pa shook his head. "Nope," he said. "The law's the law. My family is my business. I don't mess with your job, Sheriff, and I don't expect you to mess in mine."

The sheriff started to say something, then changed his mind, and we drove the rest of the way in silence. But when we got there, Tubby Watson was gone. The sheriff looked up the manager, Hank Telford, but Telford said that he had been looking for Tubby for a half hour and hadn't found him. He picked up the microphone and placed a call over the loudspeakers for Watson, but he didn't show up. The vet did, however, and said he saw Watson climb into his pickup, a blue '48 Ford with the tailgate wired on, and drive out of the lot about the time we had left. The sheriff and Pa exchanged looks, and the sheriff nodded.

"Reckon there might be something more to it than circumstance," Frost said. "I'll put out an all-points on him for questioning." He paused. "You want, I can send a deputy out to your place with you."

Pa shook his head. "Ain't no need for that. We kill our own snakes out there. You just catch him and check that out. He may have gotten beat up, but there was no sense in killing a man over something like that. But Watson"—he shook his head—"Watson's just plain mean. He comes back on our place, we'll let you know."

"Before or after?" Frost said unblinkingly.

Pa stared hard at him. "Why, that depends upon him, don't it?"

Mom tried to take the gloom off the day as we drove across the Missouri River into Pierre to finish our shopping. She laughed and tried to play the remember-when game, but Pa just grunted at her questions, and I was too young to make a good stab at it. Still, she tried, and when we got to Pierre, she insisted that we all go into the Corner Drugstore to have a soda at the fountain before we tended to the rest of our shopping. I guess mothers have an instinct for what it takes to shake a person out of the doldrums, because after we had our sodas—mine was cherry—and Pa had licked the last of the chocolate off his spoon, he perked up and said that he noticed that a John Wayne movie, *Three Godfathers*, was playing at the State Theater in honor of Christmas along with another rerun that was one of Pa's favorites, *Red River*, and he reckoned that since we were in town, we might as well make a full night of it. Mom looked startled for a moment; then Pa grinned and caught her up around her waist and planted a kiss plumb on her lips.

"Tom!" she exclaimed. Flustered, she touched her hair while others around her grinned at her embarrassment.

"It's Christmas," Pa said, then pointed above her head at the mistletoe dropping down from the high ceiling on a string. " 'Sides, you were standing under it. Tradition, you know."

She laughed and tucked her arm under his and guessed that she could make an exception this one time for his public display, given the season and all. She looked down at me and said that we would meet at the Liberty Café in two hours for dinner and handed me ten dollars to do some last-minute shopping myself, nodding her head as she reminded me that I had to buy Rose Marie's present yet and she just knew that Rose Marie wanted the Miss Angel doll at Woolworth's. I started to protest that someone might see me buying a doll, but Mom's eyebrows drew together and I shut up, knowing that she need only one more excuse to give me another lecture on the meaning of Christmas. Instead, I sighed and nodded and said that I would get around to it; then I promised when I saw that the thundercloud wasn't lifting any from her face. Pa grinned and handed me another couple of dollars and suggested that I might want to lay in a couple of boxes of cartridges as we might do a little coyote hunting or at least help reduce the prairie dog population some on the south pasture.

We left the drugstore and I started to turn to walk down the hill to the flats when Mom paused and said that she had an appointment that she needed to take care of. I didn't think much about it, but Pa gave her a strange look and asked if she would be all right. She smiled and told us to get on with our shopping and that she would find us after she was finished. She turned and left us, and Pa stared at her back for a moment as she took off toward the clinic. Then he threw his arm over my shoulder.

We walked down the hill together to the downtown on the flats. I stayed on the north side of the street while he crossed over. I wandered into Red's Sporting Goods and stared at the guns and knives he had out on display and bought a couple of boxes of .22 Long Rifles. I walked on down past the Rexall Drug Store, then slipped inside and bought the newest issues of *The Rawhide Kid* and *Kid Colt* and a pack of Beech-Nut chewing gum. I strolled the street toward the river, stopping to visit with Oly Anderson for a minute, then crossed the light and went on down to the western shop, where I glanced around carefully for Pa before darting inside and buying a pair of deerskin gloves I had seen Pa try on near Thanksgiving and a small turquoise pin worked into the shape of a turtle that I thought Mom might like.

I sighed and crossed over the street and walked back up the other side to the Woolworth's store. Wasn't anything but to get on with it and hope that no one who knew me saw me buying that damn doll that Rose Marie wanted for Christmas. I already had a pair of socks for Rose Marie's father and a handkerchief for Aunt Flo. Grandpa had a new hula-popper bass plug under the Christmas tree for him, and a set of lilac sachets for Grandma had been bought on sale in Phillip when we went there one Saturday. Stocker was getting a new braided leather hatband for the good hat he wore when he went "shoo-flying." So once I had that doll, I was pretty well done with my Christmas shopping.

I walked in and peeked down the aisle where the girl stuff was set out on display. Nobody I knew was down that aisle. I stuck my hands into my pockets and walked down, pretending a casualness I really didn't feel, then paused just opposite the Miss Angel doll. I took another quick look around, then grabbed the doll and headed for the front of the store, hoping that I could get it bought and in a sack before anyone saw me with it.

My luck didn't hold, though. Fast Teddy caught me at the cash register waiting in line with that doll in my hands. I didn't like Fast Teddy; you really couldn't trust him past the moment. That is, once you were out of sight, he thought that whatever you had told him in confidence was his to spread around to others. He was skinny as a rail and vain as a rooster about his oiled black locks, which he combed up into a pompadour like Elvis Presley's.

"Well, well," he said, a big grin splitting his thin face. "Whatcha got there, *Samantha?* You playing house now instead of pretending to be a boy?"

"Watch your mouth, Teddy," I warned him. I placed the doll up on the counter. "Just so happens that I'm getting this for my cousin. Christmas, you know."

"Sure, sure," he said, and winked. He poked me in the shoulder with a dirty forefinger. "And we all know that you ain't one of them sissies like Ennis Hancock, right? Or maybe you an' him are gonna play house?"

Now, that was about the last straw. Ennis Hancock, one of the janitors at Pierre High School, had been found in the broom closet next door to the girls' locker room where he had bored a small hole in the wall. When they caught him, he had his pants down around his ankles. At least, that was what I had overheard Ross Thurman telling Pa when he thought I wasn't in the barn back in September while we were doing the fall branding.

I turned away from the counter and stepped close to Fast Teddy, staring him full in the eye. He looked uneasy and tried to step back, but I came up in front of him again and grabbed the front of his blue parka so he couldn't move away.

"Now, you want to explain just what you meant by that last crack?" I asked him softly.

"Lemme go," he said, and tried to push my hand away.

"Well?" I demanded, feeling the tension building in me.

"What's going on here?"

I cringed, recognizing Mom's voice, and let loose of my grip on Teddy's parka. He scurried away, looking over his shoulder to make sure that I wasn't following him. He paused and shot me the bird with his middle finger before he ducked down the aisle, heading for the door. I shook my head and turned back to the counter. I glanced up at Mom's stern face staring down at me.

"Oh, nothing," I said. I gave a hollow laugh. "You know Teddy. He's always running off at the mouth before he puts his brain in gear. He started making comments about me buying this stupid doll."

"And you couldn't overlook it, that right?" Mom asked.

I glanced around at the grins of the people who stood in line behind us and turned away, my ears reddening.

"Mom," I said softly. "People are looking." But the words seemed to have no effect on her this time, although we usually had our confrontations in private.

"It's Christmas," she scolded. "That means you think about other people for a change and not yourself. Now, it doesn't hurt you one bit to overlook other people's narrow-mindedness. Oh, why do I bother? I don't think you're ever going to make a little lady."

And I knew I was in for it later. That "why do I bother" line always signaled worse to come, and I had only made the mistake once of sassing her back with "darned if I know"— a smart-alec comment that caught me a slap that made my ears ring. I did the next best thing I could under the circumstances: I lied.

"Sorry," I mumbled, trying my damnedest to look contrite. "I guess I wasn't thinking."

She glanced at me suspiciously for a long moment until the girl at the cash register took the doll and rung it up. I paid and took the sack and walked outside with her.

"Where's Pa?" I asked, trying to change the subject.

"Over at J. C. Penney's," she said absently. I looked up at her. She was staring across the street at Mrs. Six Feathers and her daughter coming out of the Rexall Drug Store. Mrs. Six Feathers carried a small sack in one hand. The girl—Sarah, I remembered—looked across the street at us, and I could feel the hard glare of her eyes even at that distance. Mrs. Six Feathers opened the door of the old pickup and helped Sarah inside. She moved stiffly, and I remembered what the sheriff had said about what had happened to her.

"I guess there isn't going to be much of a Christmas in that house," Mom said as Mrs. Six Feathers backed out carefully and drove down the street, turning the corner toward the bridge. She shook her head sadly. A tear came to her eye. "That poor little girl," she said. She sighed and looked down at me and her mouth tightened. "Count yourself lucky," she said. "That could have happened to you, the way you're always hanging around with the boys and the men instead of other girls." She started to say something else, but I saw Pa come out of J. C. Penney's and cross against the light.

"Here comes Pa," I said, interrupting her. I knew she would be upset at the interruption, but I would rather take that later than now. There was always the chance she would forget what she was about to say or even that she had something to say. That didn't happen very often but often enough to give me an eighty-twenty chance, and that was better than a hundred to one.

The Oldsmobile headlights carved a narrow white tunnel through the darkness as Pa drove us back to the ranch over the Bad River Road, slowing slightly to go through Ithaca. He turned off on Ash Creek Road and slowed carefully. Lope Stone had hit an antelope along this same road a couple of years back and damned near killed himself when the antelope flew headfirst through the windshield, nearly impaling him with its horns. As it was, he carried a nasty scar on his left cheek that drew his lips up in a grim snarl. I kept watch along the road, trying to peer through the inky black. I leaned my forehead against the window pane on the passenger side and shaded my eyes to cut the glare from the dashboard. Shadows of fence posts flickered by, and occasionally I saw a black blob that I thought to be a cow but my imagination quickly built into something deadly and evil. For some strange reason I remembered a comic book story about a ghoul who supplied bodies to a doctor for his experimentation. When the ghoul ran out of freshly buried bodies, he began to supply fresh bodies. The doctor didn't want to be a part of this, but he still needed to experiment and so reluctantly continued his association with the ghoul. Then, when the doctor finally married, his experiments ceased to matter to him and he told the ghoul that he would buy no more bodies from him. The ghoul told the doctor that he would live to regret this decision. Two nights later when the doctor returned to his house, he found his wife's head spiked to the front door. And for some strange reason, the night suddenly became ominous and threatening, and I drew away from the cold window to put the glass solidly between me and the darkness.

The bridge crossing Bad River was icy, and Pa slid carefully across, slowing to a snail's pace. I looked down through the reflected sweep of Pa's headlights; the river showed dark and sinister beneath the ice. I shivered as I thought about the car sliding off the bridge and dropping beneath the cold water. Then we were across the bridge and Pa relaxed as he drove on south to the ranch.

Pa dropped us off at the house and drove down to the shed we used as a garage. I followed Mom into the house and took her coat, hanging it up in the closet along with mine. She eyed me seriously, and I sighed inwardly, knowing what was coming.

"We need to talk," she said quietly. She pressed her fingers against her stomach in a gesture that had become familiar by now.

A recklessness came over me. Suddenly I was tired of her grousing at me, of her complaints that I was trying to be something that I wasn't, of every tiny little thing that seemed to make her angry at me.

"Yeah, maybe we do," I said hotly. "You keep saying that I'm embarrassing you all the time. Why can't you just leave me alone? I don't think you had any call to take me on that way at Woolworth's tonight. I hadn't done nothing. That was just—just—kid stuff, you know?"

Her eyes narrowed as she studied me. "There are times when you have to start thinking about not being a kid," she began. "I'm sorry if—"

"Mom," I said, interrupting her, "can we just forget it? It's Christmas Eve. Let's just open the presents and forget it.

I don't think I'm ever going to satisfy you. I can't help it if I was born a girl." I started toward the Christmas tree, intending on sorting them out as I always did.

"Samantha," she said quietly. I stopped and turned back to her. "There are some things that you need to understand." She pressed her hands against her stomach. "Some things you need to know whether you want to know them or not. Christmas Eve can wait for a few minutes. I need to tell you something."

"Why does everything I want to do always have to wait?" I blurted.

She looked startled for a moment, then her lips thinned out into a line I knew all too well. I sighed again, knowing I had stepped over my bounds. I shouldn't have gotten too cocky when she said she was sorry.

"You'd better get to bed," she said seriously. She rubbed the tired lines under her smudged eyes and grimaced.

"But it's Christmas Eve," I blurted without thinking. "We always open presents on Christmas Eve."

"I think," she said slowly, "that you need to understand that Christmas isn't simply for presents and the world doesn't revolve around what you want. Other people need to have a say in its doings. I think you'd better think about that for the night. Then, in the morning, you tell me what you think Christmas means and then *maybe*"—she emphasized—"*maybe* we'll have our Christmas. Now, go on upstairs to bed."

I recognized the finality of her words and turned despondently toward the stairs. Pa walked into the tension, his shoulders lightly dusted with snow, his cheery face wreathed in a smile. "Well," he said, clapping his hands together, then shrugging off his coat, "it looks as if we are going to have a white Christmas."

Then the smile slipped from his face as he saw me standing glumly at the stairway.

"What's going on?" he asked quietly.

"Some of us need to remember what Christmas is about," Mom said. She pressed the palm of her hand against her stomach.

He glanced at me, then back at her. "And?"

"I have decided that we will think about celebrating Christmas tomorrow," she said with finality.

His eyes tightened. "Don't you think we should have talked about this? And why don't you let up on Sam? You have been going on about the meaning of Christmas for about a month now, browbeating her with these grand pronouncements of yours about the meaning of Christmas. I think you've had your nose in Reverend Boskins's church so long that you are beginning to think like him. Christmas doesn't begin and end in that church. It's only a small part of it."

"He's a good man," she said defensively, her chin going up against Pa's words.

"He's a damn hypocrite," Pa said flatly.

She stared at him silently for a long moment, then turned and walked past me. "You do what you want," she said.

"This ain't about Sam, is it?" he asked. She stared at him. "You heard something at the doctor's office, didn't you?"

I thought I caught a glimpse of tears before she made a brief nod and turned without speaking to climb the stairs.

Pa sighed and looked at me. We stared at each other for a long moment, then he shook his head and said, "Well, Sam, I guess you'd better get off to bed after all. We'll celebrate

Christmas in the morning. Maybe she'll feel better then."

"Pa," I said. He stared at me, waiting. "Is there something wrong with Mom?"

Tears glinted in his eyes as he turned quickly and walked up the stairs away from me. At the top, he paused and looked back down at me. For a brief moment I felt him reach across the distance separating us and felt his affection. A sad smile touched his lips; then he turned and disappeared. I listened to his boots clumping down the hall and the creak of the bedroom door opening and closing. And silence.

I sighed and went into the living room and stared at the presents heaped beneath the Christmas tree. Normally we would be opening some of them now to give us a family Christmas before Grandma and Grandpa came in from Fort Pierre on Christmas Day and Aunt Flo and Uncle Jimmy came in from Rapid City, all bringing their additions to the gift giving. A great silence fell upon the house, and I listened to the sounds of the house giving itself over to the night. I crossed to the radio and turned it on low, slumping over the red hassock as Lionel Barrymore's rich voice came handily over the hiss and crackle of the airwaves. I lay back, listening to the familiar story of Charles Dickens's *A Christmas Carol*; that rebroadcast was now pretty traditional. But this time, I heard the story and heard the spirits as they worked hard to save the decrepit soul of the despicable miser, and I listened thoughtfully, remembering Mom's words that she hoped I would figure out what Christmas was. I already had a good idea what it wasn't—it wasn't the presents heaped under the tree and it wasn't the lights. And I really didn't think it was anything Reverend Boskins said, despite what Mom would like to believe. I didn't think it was the church, either. But I was hanged if I could figure out just what it was Mom kept hinting at.

I listened carefully to the story, trying to unravel the conundrum that Mom had presented to me before going to bed, but whatever it was, it kept eluding me. I guess my mind really wasn't on it full-time and all as I kept thinking back to what Pa had said just before he climbed the stairs to bed. Somehow I guess I knew that me needing to find out about the true meaning of Christmas was only part of the reason that we weren't opening presents that night. There was something else about Mom that I hadn't been told. Something not so good. But Mom and Pa always kept pretty quiet about their aches and pains unless it was obvious, and even then they ignored their hurts mostly.

I rolled off the hassock and lay on my back, watching the bubble lights on the tree. Come to think of it, Mom and Pa really didn't tell me much. Most stuff I had to figure out for myself, like now. I sighed and turned over on my stomach, listening halfheartedly to the show, poking one of the presents in front of me. I rose and walked into the hallway where I had left the presents I had bought and took them out of their sacks. I had talked the salesgirl in the western store into wrapping the gloves and pin, so now I had only the doll to wrap. I opened the closet and took out a roll of Christmas paper and Scotch tape and ribbon and wrapped it the best I could. I placed the presents under the tree and stood staring at them. I knew why we gave presents on Christmas—Reverend Boskins pointed that out each year in his sermon on the three wise men—and I knew that we made too much a hoopla over imitating the wise men and their gift giving. I also knew about Christ's birthday and all that, and I was grateful to him for having been born and all. I wasn't stupid; I had caught that connection. But I knew that that wasn't what Mom was talking about at all. Nothing was ever that simple with her.

At last the show came to an end, and I turned off the radio and removed my boots to tiptoe upstairs. I undressed and quickly crawled into bed, shivering in the cold. I took a comic book from the pile beneath my bed, then put it back and reached again and pulled out Zanc Grey's *The Last Trail* and began reading about Deathwind and Jonathon Zane as they started to track down Leggett and the sailor who had stolen the woman that Jonathon loved. But the story didn't hold my interest after the first few pages, and I put the book-mark back in place and put the book on the table beside my bed. I stared across the room at the bookstand in the corner and got up out of bed and crossed to it. I took a copy of Bret Harte stories about the Old West and went back to bed, shiv-ering as I crawled beneath the sheets and snuggled under the heavy comforter. I opened the book to the table of contents and glanced through it, searching for a short piece. My eyes fell on "How Santa Claus Came to Simpson's Bar," and I turned to it and began reading about the ride of Dick Bullen and how he had spurred the half-wild Jovita across country to buy toys for a little boy who was going to have a barren Christmas.

"I guess there isn't going to be much of a Christmas in that house."

I looked up from my book, staring at the door. The words had come so loudly that they seemed as if they had just been spoken. A warmth suddenly seeped through me, and I saw again Abel's battered pickup truck pulling away from the J. C. Penney's store in Pierre and turning down the highway toward the steel-girded bridge arching over the Missouri River. And I saw the girl's eyes—Sarah, yes, that was her name—staring at me from the window of the truck. Her eyes grew bigger and bigger, and then I heard Mom's voice creeping through the dark to me: "That poor little girl. That could've been you."

I laid my book down and stared out the window on my left at our yard light burning brightly in the dark. I couldn't see any stars or the moon. I thought about the lights strung on evergreen garlands swagging across the streets in Pierre and Fort Pierre and on our tree downstairs, and I wondered if Abel had managed to get a Christmas tree for his family before he was killed.

And then I thought I knew the meaning of Christmas, and a lump formed in my throat. I lay thinking for a moment; then I rose and quietly crossed to my dresser. I opened the bottom drawer and pulled out a long-handled union suit and slipped into it. I sat on my bed and pulled on two pairs of socks and my jeans, then took a Tom Sawyer flannel shirt from the drawer and buttoned it full against my neck, tucking it into my jeans. I found a woolen scarf that my aunt had given to me a couple of years before and wrapped it twice around my neck. Then, taking my boots in hand, I crept down the hall, pausing beside Mom and Pa's door, listening to their heavy night breathing. I took a deep breath and went downstairs, stepping over the third step that creaked loudly whenever anyone stepped on it.

I went out onto the porch and opened the closet where Mom kept her cleaning supplies. I found a couple of burlap gunnysacks in the closet and shook them out gingerly, pinching my nose to keep from sneezing from the fine sift of oat

dust that powdered the air. I went into the living room and
turned on the Christmas lights. I looked up at the porcelain
angel sitting on top of the Christmas tree, her wings out-
stretched, a tiny halo of lights circling her fine blond hair. The
warmth returned to the pit of my stomach, and I looked
down at the presents heaped beneath the tree. I hesitated, then
pulled out the presents to me and Rose Marie and carefully
removed the name tags. I put Rose Marie's in one gunnysack,
pulled the drawstring taut, and tied a red ribbon around the
mouth of the sack. I didn't know what they were, but I knew
they would be for a girl. I had to open my presents just
enough to see what they were. I had to set two from Grandma
(a frilly blouse and plaid skirt) and one from my uncle and
aunt (a yellow sweater), and one from Mom (a blue dress with
a white collar) aside. Then I thought, they'd do for her, too,
and untied the red ribbon and stuck them inside along with
the others and retied the sack. The others—a pair of spurs
from Dad, a new pair of leather chaps from Grandpa, jeans
and flannel shirts, a couple of *Lash LaRue* and *Hopalong Cas-
sidy* comic books, Zane Grey's *The Maverick Queen* and *The
Dude Ranger*, a pair of leather cuff guards—went into the
other sack and I tied that one with a green ribbon. I carried
them out to the porch and set them down by the door. I
shrugged into my parka and pulled a knit stocking cap down
over my ears. I pulled my cowboy hat down firmly over the
stocking cap. I started to pull on my fur-lined gloves, then
hesitated and went back to the living room. I began to per-
spire in the heat. I found the pin I had bought Mom and
dropped it into the side pocket of my parka. I looked around
again, noticed the small artificial Christmas tree with the tiny
balls and star on top setting on the piano. I took it out to the

porch, opened a gunnysack, dropped the tree in, then retied the bag. I went back into the living room, glanced around again, then turned off the Christmas lights and left.

Out on the porch, I took my .22 rifle from the rack beside the door and Pa's saddle sheath and placed the rifle inside it. I dropped a handful of cartridges into a side pocket of my coat. Then I tied the gunnysacks together by the drawstrings and draped them over my shoulder, staggering from the sudden swing of their weight. I caught myself, then opened the door and stepped out into the cold night.

I paused, shivering and shaking by the boot blade for scraping away mud, while my eyes adjusted to the dark. My breath came in a fine mist, hanging in the cold briefly like a tiny cloud. I walked down to the barn, staggering awkwardly from the bulk and swing of the gunnysacks.

Spotty sensed me when I entered the barn and grumbled loudly as if he knew the night ride ahead of him. I hung the gunnysacks over a baling hook and went into the tack shed to get my saddle, blanket, and bridle. Pale moonlight streaked in through the dirty windowpanes. I felt Abel's presence although he had been gone for four days. I hurried out of there and back to Spotty's stall. He protested as I stepped in beside him and slipped the bridle over his head.

"Quiet," I ordered. I smoothed the blanket over his back and lifted the saddle on. He shuffled his hooves unhappily and grunted when I drew the cinch tight.

I led him out of the stall and took my rifle in the sheath and strapped it on with the stock lifting up behind the saddle. Then I checked the knot tying the two gunnysacks together and draped them over the pommel like saddlebags. I mounted awkwardly and rode out of the barn, pausing to swing the door shut behind me.

I took a deep breath and rode out of the ranch yard. I planned to take the long way along the river road, but I saw the lights of a pickup coming toward me and rode back into the yard. The pickup slowed by our gate and I saw it—a battered blue Ford pickup—and I rode behind the corral and south, following the route Abel had taken on his last ride.

"Never mind," I said softly to Spotty. "It'll be faster this way." Spotty grumbled and I touched him gently with my heels, riding through the gate.

Chapter VIII

We went across the south pasture to where the gully sliced through on its way to the loop of Bad River where it nearly doubled back on itself in an oxbow.

We rode through the brush. Spotty snorted unhappily as he floundered through the thin ice that covered the gentle trickle of the spring cutting through the bottom of the gully and seeping around the roots of the chokecherry bushes. The black and withered arms of the plum trees stretched gnarled fingers to the sky. Boa-like skiffs of snow draped over their tops. The moon and stars failed to light the way. A great weariness filled me, and I wished the leaves were turning again in autumn and the air was filled with the smoky taste of moldering leaves, but all I felt was a blue breeze blowing across my back and the rattle of branches like bones when the bushes and trees felt the push of the wind. And I heard whispers on the wind that lifted the tiny hairs on my neck. The moon crept a silver disk from beneath the cloud covering, then darted back beneath a darker, more ominous cloud. I looked behind—a quick glance only—and saw a barren wasteland of white, glittering like tiny diamonds. I shivered and huddled deeper into my parka. The two gunnysacks bumped awkwardly against my knees.

Then I felt it—a gentle pushing against my body. I felt it first against my face, then my back and chest at once. For a moment I was puzzled; then Spotty shook his head and glanced around uneasily, and I remembered Pa telling me that cows and horses knew a change of weather was coming long before a human. I felt the chill as if the bottom had dropped out of the thermometer. A coyote howled, and Spotty nickered deep in his throat. Uneasily I reached back and touched the stock of my .22 rifle in the sheath beneath my leg for reassurance.

Spotty scrambled up the wall of the gully, his hooves digging gouts of frozen clay out of the wall as he scrambled out on top. He snorted with displeasure, and I lifted the reins, nudging him gently with my heels. The frost-rimed grass crackled beneath his hooves.

A numbness set over me, and I knotted the reins and draped them over the saddle horn. I slapped my arms together. Spotty jerked his head, startled. Then he settled back into his trot across the pasture. I wrapped my arms around myself, rubbing the cold from my ribs. Spotty reached the barbed wire, and I turned him south, following it down to Bad River. The willows looked like silver lace. I studied the black water flowing under the ice, then decided that the ice wouldn't hold Spotty's weight and turned his nose, riding for the narrow bridge stretched across the river.

Once across the bridge, the wire stretched down for three miles before cutting smartly away toward the east and west, and there the vast emptiness of the land stretched out toward the Badlands, forming the Pine Ridge Indian Reservation. The land appeared so transparent I could hear it ticking in the crystalline cold. Plum Creek lay straight in front of us, and there I would turn southwest and ride on into Abel's small single-loop ranch. As if he sensed the near end of our journey, Spotty's pace quickened. Large flakes of snow began to fall, but I knew it wouldn't fall fast enough to bother us going. The problem would be coming back. If we didn't hurry, we could be caught out in the prairie. Visions of Abel frozen beside our fence flickered across my mind. I stood up in the stirrups and stretched, trying to remove the memory. An icy wind sprang up and the willows darkened against the snow. The cold made my toes rattle in my boots.

Behind the clouds the stars burned with a lidless fixity. Spotty scrambled over a wash of pebbles sprinkled with blue ice. All the land lay cold and white, with blue-black shadows patched across the whiteness. In places the snow lay in deep pockets, and Spotty floundered through them. We crossed a clay wash and moved out onto the arctic prairie. Spotty's breath came in misty clouds and a CHUFF! CHUFF! as he moved steadily across the white expanse. Sparse tufts of grama grass showed like yellowed ivory in patches where the wind had swept the snow away.

Plum Creek came in front of us, and Spotty turned automatically, his pace lifting again until I was forced to hold him down to keep him from sweating from his effort. A light flickered in the darkness ahead. Relief swept over me and I felt the tension ease from my shoulders, the stiffness from my back.

I almost fell as I stepped stiffly from the saddle. I tied Spotty to a horseshoe ring hanging from a post planted a few feet from the door. I pulled my gloves off and fumbled at the knots holding the gunnysacks to my saddle. They gave way suddenly and I staggered under their sudden weight. I caught them on my shoulders and stumbled to the door. I kicked at the screen until a light suddenly flashed on above my head, causing me to blink in its brightness. I kicked at the door again. The door opened cautiously. A black eye stared over a bright chain at me.

"Hi," I croaked. I swallowed painfully. "Merry Christmas."

After a brief hesitation, she closed the door. I heard the chain rattle; then the door opened wide and she stepped aside. I entered and eased the gunnysacks to the floor. The sudden warmth of the room made me ache. I took a deep breath, smelling wood smoke and beneath that a hint of fuel oil.

"What are you doing out on a night like this?" she demanded as she closed and locked the door behind me. She caught me staring at the lock and her chin went up defensively. "We have to do that, now. Especially after—" Her voice caught in her throat, and she swallowed for a second, looking away from me but not before I caught a tear sliding down her cheek. She took a deep breath and turned back.

"After Abel's death?" I asked.

She looked at me closely, then nodded. "Yes, that's right. After Abel's death. That man is still out there somewhere."

"Tubby Watson," I said.

She glanced at me curiously. Then her eyes widened as she realized what I had said.

"You know who?"

I nodded. "Yeah. I saw him using Abel's knife at the sale barn in Fort Pierre. You mean no one told you?"

She shook her head. A bitter smile twisted the corners of her mouth, and the skin tightened over her face. "No. They don't tell Indians anything."

"But you're not Indian!" I blurted; then my face burned and I looked away. "Sorry," I mumbled. "I didn't mean nothing about that."

"You can't help being you," she said. "You are what they made you. In my case, it isn't who I am; it's who I married that made me what I am to them."

"Huh?" I said, confused. She shrugged wearily and moved away from the door and into the room.

"You'll understand when you're older. If you remember," she added. "It doesn't matter one way or the other, really. Times change and some people change. You might. Then again, you might not." She looked at me again. "You're Mr. McCaslin's girl, aren't you? What are you doing out on a night like this?"

I nudged the gunnysacks with the toe of my boot. "I brought this stuff over," I said.

She looked at it curiously. "What is it?"

Suddenly I felt embarrassed and looked away. My nose began to run, and I wiped it on the sleeve of my parka. "Well," I said, "I know that Abel didn't have time to get into Pierre or Phillip to get what he wanted for Christmas, so I just thought that . . . well, that is, I wanted to—Merry Christmas!" I blurted.

Her face softened a bit. "You mean you brought presents over here for Sarah and Tommy?"

"Yes, ma'am," I said, shifting from one foot to the other. My face felt hot again and I looked away from her. "That is, well, I don't believe in Santa Claus or nothing like that anymore, but that don't mean that Sarah and Tommy don't. And if they do, well, it would be too bad if he didn't come this year just because of what happened to Abel and everything. Mrs. Six Feathers, it just ain't right for that to happen! None of it! So I just thought—"

"Where did you get the presents?" she asked suddenly.

"Doesn't matter." A grin tugged at my lips. "Santa's workshop. Ain't that where they come from?"

A smile brightened the tired lines in her face and tears filled her eyes. I looked away, embarrassed. She came over and stood looking down at me, then bent and kissed me, and I felt embarrassed.

"You're worth them all put together," she said softly.

"Huh?" I asked.

"Never mind," she began, but I interrupted her.

"I know, I'll understand when I get older. Yes, ma'am, maybe I will. And then maybe I can explain it better."

"I don't think it can be explained any better," she said, wiping the tears from her eyes with the tip of her shawl. "You know, we had a lot of hope after what your father did at the dance." I frowned in confusion. "You know—when he stood up for Abel and such against the others."

I shook my head. "That wasn't anything. It was just something that had to be done."

"No," she said softly, tears streaking down her cheeks again. "No, it didn't. At least not with an Indian it didn't. And it wouldn't have except for your father. He gave us a lot of hope by what he did. Hope that maybe things were going to be for the better, and maybe we wouldn't be just Indians anymore. But—"

She sniffed and looked down at the gunnysacks. "We don't have a tree to put them under," she said.

"Yes, ma'am, you do," I said, gesturing at the sack that had Rose Marie's doll in it. "It ain't much, but it'll do, I guess, in a pinch."

She bent and untied the green ribbon and opened the sack and took out the small tinseled tree with the tiny balls and tiny star on top. One of the tiny Christmas balls had broken, and the tinsel had knotted on one side, and one of the plastic icicles had fallen off, but for all of that, it still looked pretty good. She took it to a small table by the armchair and took the reading lamp off and placed the tree on it, then stepped back, looking at it.

"I guess it ain't so hot, is it?" I asked. I rubbed my nose again. "But it's all I could bring on Spotty."

She turned and looked at me. "You rode your horse all the way over here from the ranch?" she said wonderingly. She shook her head. "I can't believe it. You're just like your father."

Well, that confused me a bit and made me squirm as my face got all hot and everything. I could tell she was on the verge of crying again, so I just up and said, "Yes, ma'am. Well, that wasn't so bad and it ain't as far as it sounds. I came cross-country, so that shortened it a bit."

She stared at me for a long time, until I felt myself growing hot again and covered my embarrassment by reaching into the sack and taking out the doll. The bow was crushed and one corner of the wrapping had torn. I held it out to her and said, "Well, this one's for Sarah. I don't know if it's what she wanted or not, but it's the best that I could do. It's Miss Angel."

"The new one," she said. It wasn't a question, but I nodded anyway.

"There's a bit of other stuff in there, too," I said. "And this here sack's for Tommy," I said, nudging the other one with the toe of my boot. I hoped she wouldn't ask me what it was 'cause I didn't have the slightest idea what was there and I didn't want her to know that they were my presents.

"I didn't know his size and all, so I had to guess, you know. And well, shucks, it's all guesswork, ain't it?"

She stared at me for a second. "These your presents?" she asked quietly.

"Ma'am?" I fumbled, looking for an answer. I stuck my hand in my pocket and felt the pin and pulled it out and handed it to her. "This one's for you."

Tears gathered in her eyes, and I glanced away, embarrassed for her, at the door. "You know, I really gotta get going. It's starting to snow and I wanna get back before it hits. Gonna be a big one. I can feel it coming," I added. I turned and walked to the door, pulling my gloves on again. For the first time I realized how warm it was in that place, and a great tiredness suddenly fell upon me like a warm and fuzzy blanket. I forced myself not to yawn. "I really hope you all have a good Christmas, ma'am," I said.

"Now, hold on," she said. "You can't go out there with that storm coming down. You can stay here."

"No, ma'am," I said. "I really have to get back."

"No, and there's an end to it," she said firmly, taking a step toward me. The door opened behind her and Sarah walked out, rubbing her eyes.

"Mommy," she said. "I had a bad dream."

She turned and crossed hurriedly to Sarah and bent and took her in her arms. "It's all right," she said softly. Sarah looked over her shoulder at me, her eyes big and soft. I felt myself begin to sink in their depths and reached behind me for the doorknob. I slipped the lock and turned the doorknob quietly and stepped out, easing the door shut behind me.

I hurried to Spotty and untied him from the ring and stepped into the saddle. He grunted and mouthed his bit, but

I pulled him away from the house and touched my heels to his sides. I heard the door open and her voice, but the rising wind whipped the words away, and I galloped away into the night.

Chapter IX

✦ ✦ ✦ And the wind grew and the snow fell heavier and whipped around in the wind, creating small maelstroms on the high ground that momentarily blinded me. I let the reins slacken, looping them around the horn, trusting to Spotty's instinct and to give him free rein if he suddenly stumbled. I didn't want to be left out in the storm alone if he broke his leg.

And then the adventure disappeared and I became afraid. I felt as if I was in the middle of a whiteout, the falling snow being the only clue I had for direction. The wind, I knew, came from the north, and I turned into it, keeping our faces full into it. Then, I became aware of the wind whipping from north by northwest to north and knew that we were in trouble. Spotty followed the fence line down into a gully that I knew opened into a wash on the other side of the pasture. From there, we could follow the fence line over to Anderson's place, cut through his old wheat field, and pick up the road to cross the bridge over Bad River. Then it would be a simple trip along the road to our home gate. Simple. I nearly laughed. On a clear day it might be simple, but this was not a clear day, and "simple" had been drifted over by the snow.

We rode down the gully and into the plum thicket. I breathed a sigh of relief. Down here, we were protected from the wind, and the snow, although falling heavily with thick flakes like cotton puffs, was manageable. I ducked beneath the heavy limb of an Osage orange tree.

And then I felt evil come with a rush like fast water or a sudden gust of wind, carrying with it a sudden bad-smelling emptiness. A coyote slipped across the brush in front of us. Spotty shied suddenly, throwing me to the right, and I lurched in the saddle, catching myself by the saddle horn. Something whacked into the tree branch where my head had been, sending a shower of snow over me. I heard a low, flat crack. Spotty jumped again, and something slammed again into the tree beside me. I heard the low, flat crack again and suddenly realized that someone was shooting. Automatically I reached behind and grabbed my rifle and kicked my feet free from the stirrups, threw my leg over the saddle, and slid to the ground. A bullet whanged off a rock and I sprawled behind the Osage orange. Spotty reared and galloped away down the wash.

"Hey! I ain't no damn deer!" I hollered, and immediately ducked back behind the Osage orange as a bullet whanged off the trunk. I began to shiver and my teeth chattered. I had to pee and my mouth suddenly felt dry. I rubbed my tongue against the roof of my mouth and tried again.

"Hey! I ain't a deer!"

The tree vibrated as a bullet slammed into it, and I squirmed, trying to work my way deeper into the ground, but my coat and zipper was in the way. I felt light-headed and realized that I was panting. I swallowed painfully and forced myself to breathe slower. Too many shots had been fired now for this to be an accident. The first couple could have been fired when a hunter was looking for a deer and saw Spotty's legs moving in the snow flurries. Even though deer season was over, poachers wouldn't pay any attention to the law, and I was close enough to the reservation that a couple of Indians might have been out taking advantage of the snow to bulk out their larder. But no Indian would waste as much ammunition as whoever was firing now. One shot, possibly two, but that would be it. Not—how many had it been? I tried to recall and another slammed into the trunk. I peeked around the bole. A sudden wind cleared the swirling snow for a moment, and I saw what looked like the shape of a hat on top of the gully where it looped around in a bend to the north. Then again, maybe it was only a bush. The snow closed in again and I pulled back behind the tree, trying to think.

I slipped my gloves off and removed my cowboy hat and gently pushed it to the left as I peered around the trunk to the right. The wind kicked the snow away again, and I saw the shape move, then a tiny spit of flame, and I heard the smack of a bullet off the frozen earth and the sharp, low crack. I pushed my rifle forward and waited a minute. The flame licked out again and I fired twice rapidly. The .22 made tiny pops like frozen twigs breaking. I fired again as the snow came around again and thought I heard a yelp of pain. Then panic hit and I fired as fast as I could until the hammer fell on an empty chamber and I rolled back behind the Osage orange, gasping for breath, feeling my temples throb. I fumbled cartridges from my pocket with numb fingers and tried to load the rifle, but the cartridges slipped from my grasp. I stuck my fingers into my mouth to warm them, then tried again, loading the rifle. I rolled back to peek around the Osage orange. Nothing moved. My throat ached and my eyes burned, and suddenly I had to move or pee my pants. A coyote howled against the wind, and I thought I saw a shadow flit across the gully in front of me.

I squirmed backward, leaving my hat on the ground, and crawled down the gully away from the tree until I made it around a small bend. Then I rose and dropped my pants and the flap of my union suit. I squatted and quickly urinated, my heart pounding. I grabbed my rifle and scurried up the side of the gully and lay on the edge, looking back down the way I came. The wind was heavier up here and snow blew in blinding swirls. Shadows danced between the swirls and I waited for a shot from one of the shadows. But none came, and then I wondered if he was creeping down along the rim of the gully, looking to get behind me.

I rolled away from the gully, crawled out a ways, then rose and, crouching as low as I could get, ran out into the storm, hugging my rifle to my chest.

Snow closed in around me, blinding me. The wind seemed to pick up in its intensity as I ran, stumbling over clumps of soapweed. I stepped in a hole and fell, sprawling, desperately clinging to my rifle. I lay gasping for a moment. I had no idea where I was. I should have come up against a fence by now, but I didn't know if I had been running in a straight line or not. Probably not, I reasoned. And I didn't want to continue running. I needed to move slowly so I didn't raise a sweat. The sweat would freeze and suck the body heat from me.

Shelter.

But where?

Go right.

I started and rolled over onto my stomach, trying to peer through the thick snow. Where had the voice come from?

Go right.

It came again.

"I can't," I whispered. "That's not the way home."

A quiet chuckle came from the white around me.

"Abel?" I asked.

The old place. Where you gathered rose hips.

"But—"

Go right.

And I rose and moved to my right, tasting brassy fear in the back of my throat. I tried to tell myself that I was going in the wrong direction, if I ran right when I left the gully. The way home lay to my left, and that was the way I should go. But what if you had been running in a circle? I argued. Then where would you be?

"Where you are," I muttered. "Lost."

I no longer remember how long I wandered in that swirling white amid the darkness. But suddenly a great timber loomed in front of me and I ran into it, whacking my head hard and falling backward, dazed. I blinked and rolled around until I could put my hand on it, then leaned up against it and smelled creosote and knew that I had found the railroad trestle spanning the small wash. I leaned my forehead against it and took a deep breath, then rose and made my way around it. I felt the wild rose canes swipe against my jeans as I moved through them. I stumbled against the rusty pump, and then the snow cleared for a moment, and I saw the old house in front of me and stumbled on numb feet toward it. I fell through the doorway and the wind moaned around the eaves in frustration at my escape.

I tried to peer through the gloom, but it was too dark. I crawled along a wall away from the wind gusting through the glassless windows until I found a corner and huddled in it. I leaned my rifle against the wall beside me and shoved my hands into the pockets of my parka. I drew a deep breath, smelling again the musty smells of earth like old iron and age and mildew. A great loneliness came over me. Weariness. Fear. The house creaked and shook in the gusts of wind and the dried canes of the old hollyhocks rubbed furiously against the weathered boards of the house, and each time I thought I heard whoever it was that had been shooting at me outside, creeping around the house. Snow rattled against the gray boards like a hundred woodpeckers. The dark in the house seemed to sear my eyes. The night grew longer and rigid with cold. I chattered and shook in the darkness until at last I had to move and I rose and walked cautiously around in tiny circles, flapping my arms, trying to work warmth into my bones until my shaking slowed to slow and steady instead of violent.

A shadowy form suddenly slipped among the shadows in the house and stopped. I felt it, then heard it sniffing the air. I stopped and remained quiet for a long time, straining to see in the darkness. Then it moved again, away from me to the other side of the house. I heard it padding and then the quiet settle of it as it dropped down.

Not a dog, I thought. No dog would be out in this. Must be a coyote.

I moved slowly back across the room and slid down in my old spot, touching my rifle reassuringly.

We sat like that, each of us staring across the room at the other, although we couldn't see—at least, I couldn't—as the night worked its way to morning. Slowly, gray light appeared, and then I could see him, lying in the corner, gaunt, ice particles gleaming in his gray coat. His head was down on his paws, but his yellow eyes stared at me, watching. I started to touch my rifle.

Leave it alone. He won't hurt you.

I started and the coyote's head came up, his muscles tensing.

Leave it alone.

"But—"

He's got as much right here as you do.

I sat and slumped in the corner and wearily dropped my head to my knees. The ache and pain of the past few weeks came over me and I felt the cold creeping in, wrapping her arms around me. I tried to push myself up, but I couldn't. I thought about who had been shooting at me, and although I didn't want to admit I had figured it out, I knew it was Tubby Watson. And I remembered what he had done to Abel's daughter.

That could have happened to you, the way you're always hanging around with the boys and the men instead of other girls.

An ache came in my throat.

And I cried.

Chapter X

I remembered Old Man Ferris telling about the time he was on a deer stand up in the Black Hills and suddenly a blue norther came down upon him and he tried to make it back to the camp but got lost in a whiteout and wandered in the Black Hills for the rest of the day, fighting the wind and the cold and the snow. He walked into camp the next day, legs spraddled and stiff from the cold, walking as if he was walking on buttered glass, and the black stubble on his face touched on the ends with white frost. He said it all had to do with the heart and he never realized it until then.

"The heart, Sam," he said to me, winking solemnly as he whittled on the bench outside the county courthouse. "It's the heart. You look into your heart, and then you know if you're gonna live or die. It is the best thing that can happen to you. Fills you with humility. And pride. And once you realize that, then you can make it. I knew I was gonna make it when the light turned gray the next day. Before that I didn't. But when the light turned gray, then I knew I had passed the test."

"What test?" I asked.

"Never you mind what test. You have to ask it, you can't be knowing it, and it won't make no sense for me to tell it to you because you wouldn't understand."

And then he relented a bit and leaned back on the bench,

frowning in recollection, and said, "It has to do with the summer and the fall—"

"Wait a minute; you said it was winter," I said, breaking in. "Ain't snowing in the summer."

And he eyed me balefully until I squirmed with embarrassment. He cleared his voice, "As I was saying: summer and the fall and *snow*"—he emphasized, staring at me, and I grew hot all over again—"and the sap-rife spring. It's the order of things, you see. The natural order. Understand?"

"Yeah," I said, easing away. "I understand."

"No you don't," he said, leaning forward. He pushed the blade of his knife gently against the wooden stick in his hand and watched the paring curl yellowly down the shaft of the stick and fall with the tiny shavings in a pile around his feet.

"But you will. Someday. It happens to us all at one time or the other."

And I remembered thinking that Old Man Ferris was crazier than a loon. It couldn't happen to everybody because everybody didn't hunt. I didn't mention this to him, however, because I didn't want him to get any more philosophical than he was. A person can only take so much philosophy on a warm day in June when the bass are jumping in a willow hole on Bad River.

But now I had time and I wiped my nose on the sleeve of my parka and stood up. My movement brought the coyote's head up across the room and I could feel his yellow eyes upon me. I started to reach for my rifle and felt him stiffen. I paused.

I felt him stiffen!

I brought my hand back and stared at him across the room. I felt strangely comfortable. I turned and looked around the room. Gray light slanted in through the cracks in the walls and the paneless windows. I felt light-headed, and although the snow still fell, the wind had dropped and sparrows were hopping among the wild rose canes, nipping at the rose hips I had left in the fall. I stood in the waning gloom and watched the world come alive through the deadness of the night.

I stepped over into a corner and went through the ritual of taking down my pants and the drop panel of my union suit and peed. I dressed again and went outside and took a deep breath. The air felt cold and good in my lungs. I thought about Tubby Watson and no longer was afraid of him, for I knew that he wasn't there anymore. I turned slowly in that dappled obscurity, looking around the old homestead. Snow crowned the rusted pump and lay heavily upon the dead limbs of the trees.

I turned and walked back into the house. I glanced at the corner; the coyote was gone. I walked over to my rifle and picked it up, brushing the damp from it with my glove. I took a deep breath and walked out of the old house and made my way through the bushes to the trestle. I pushed through the heavy drift in the wash and climbed up on the track. The wind had swept the track clean of snow and I turned east, walking toward the sunrise.

For the most part, the railroad tracks had blown free of snow, although in cutbanks the snow still lay heavy over the tracks. I had little choice but to work my way through the drifts, holding my rifle high so snow wouldn't accidentally plug the barrel. I nearly fell through the short bridge over Carlan's Wash, and by the time I got to Frenchman's Bend I was worn to a frazzle. My eyes burned from the constant glare off the white snow, and a headache jackhammered away deep inside my skull. I saw some rose hips on canes poking up through the snow and my belly growled with hunger. But I knew that I couldn't walk down off the track and through the snow to pick them. I wouldn't be able to climb the embankment back up onto the roadbed if I did. A squirrel scampered across the tracks and down a wash to a cottonwood. A jay spoke angrily at him as he swung from branch to branch. A raven sat on a fence post and eyed me as I passed.

About noon I felt faint and I began to stumble. I stopped and bent down to pick up a handful of snow to suck on, lost my balance, and fell forward onto my knees. My rifle clattered on the track beside me, but I was too tired to care if snow clogged the barrel now or not. My fingers and toes felt frozen, and my face had tiny numb spots in it. I grabbed a handful of snow and scrubbed it across my face, trying to awaken it again. I grabbed the rifle and forced myself to my feet, swaying. I wondered how far I had to go, but strangely, the distance didn't seem to matter. Wearily I pushed myself forward, concentrating on taking one wooden step at a time. Then another. I promised myself that after a hundred steps I would stop and rest, but I kept losing count and had to begin all over again.

"Sam!"

I paused, weaving, stumbling, looking for the voice. I lost my balance and sat abruptly on the tracks, my teeth coming together hard. Tiny black dots swam in my vision. A figure on horseback moved through the snow, the horse bucking its way through the drifts. For a moment fear ran through me as I thought I saw Tubby Watson, and I fumbled briefly, panicked, with my rifle. Then I recognized Stocker's sorrel and slumped forward, nearly weeping with relief. I waited while

Stocker gigged his horse up the embankment and onto the tracks. He stepped from the saddle and knelt beside me, gently taking the rifle from my numbed fingers and laying it aside.

"Hello, Stocker," I said. "I sure am glad to see you."

"Can you ride?" he asked.

"Sure," I said. My voice cracked and my throat hurt. I swallowed and tried to climb to my feet, but my legs turned to rubber and I sank back to the ground.

"That's all right," he said roughly. He bent and lifted me to my feet, steadying me. He helped me to his horse. I grabbed hold of the stirrup, holding tightly while Stocker jammed my rifle beneath the girth. Then he boosted me into the saddle. I swayed, holding tightly to the saddle horn. He swung into the saddle behind me and we rode away, back toward the ranch.

The ranch seemed deserted as we rode into the yard. Stocker reined in beside the porch and eased me from the saddle. A lone light shone in the kitchen window. I craned my head and focused on Stocker.

"Where's Mom and Pa?" I asked, then said stupidly, "It's Christmas Day. They should be getting ready for Grandma and Grandpa coming."

He looked away for a moment, then pulled my rifle from beneath the girth and locked hard fingers around my upper arm as he helped me to the porch.

"In Pierre," he said roughly. He leaned me against the door frame while he pulled the door open to the porch. "Your mother had to be taken in to the hospital."

"What?" I asked stupidly. "Hospital? What's wrong?"

"Come on," he said. He took me into the house, pausing to lean the rifle in a corner.

"Stocker," I said.

"I don't know what's wrong. Your father took your mother in to the hospital early this morning. You've made a proper mess out of this, I'll tell you that. Now you get up to your room and get out of those clothes. I'll call your father and let him know we got you back at the ranch house," Stocker said. He pulled my coat off and tossed it on a chair and gave me a gentle push toward the hallway. "You had everyone worried sick, girl. I know what you did and all, and it was a good thing. But the way you went about it was just plain wrong."

"It's Tubby Watson," I said.

He paused, staring at me. "What's that? What about Tubby Watson?"

"He tried to kill me. Spotty—"

"He's all right. He came home early this morning. I thought he'd throwed you or something; then I gotta call from Mrs. Six Feathers, who said you'd been there. I started riding back that way, looking for you."

"Tubby Watson tried to kill me," I said.

And then the room swam out of focus and I passed out.

Chapter XI

I slept a long time, finally awakening when Stocker came into my room, carrying a small tray with a cup of hot cocoa and a bowl of chicken noodle soup. He slid the tray onto the student desk under my window and drew the curtains. Gray light flooded the room. I glanced out the window; the clouds were like lead, heavy and swollen, hanging low over the horizon. I heard a horse nicker from the corral.

" 'Bout time you woke," Stocker said without turning. He shook his head. "Looks like a blue norther comin' in strong. No wind, but if it picks up then we've gotta bad one on our hands."

He turned to stare at me. Tired lines appeared deep in his leathery face, but his gray hair was oiled and combed and his red-and-white-checked flannel shirt neatly buttoned around the neck. I glanced at his hands, heavy and thick-jointed, and back at him.

"You put me in my jammas?" I asked.

He flushed and looked embarrassed, then he said, "Well, yes, ma'am, I did. But I pulled a quilt over you first. It seemed the only proper thing to do. I couldn't leave you in them wet clothes and all. Sorry."

By the time he had finished with his explanation, he was beet-red. "I didn't—well, that is—"

" 'Thanks, Stocker," I said quietly. "I appreciate it."

He looked relieved, then shook his head.

"I called your father and told him I'd found you and had you back and you seemed none the worse for wear," he said. He glanced away, his eyes watering. "Your mother ain't good."

"What's wrong?" I asked, alarmed. I sat up and swung my feet over the side of the bed, balancing on the edge while a wave of dizziness passed. I felt dried out like an old corn-husk.

He shook his head. "I ain't too sure about that. Your father is a bit quiet about everything, but I guess it has to do with her stomach." He hesitated. "I think it's cancer, Sam. But I ain't got the particulars."

"Cancer?" I sat numb, trying to focus on the word, re-membering Mom holding her stomach as she stood against the sink in the kitchen, her lips tight against the bellyache, as she called it. I remembered how she went from happy to angry in a finger snap and how the littlest thing seemed to set her off over the past six months.

"I called the sheriff and told him what you said about Tubby Watson," Stocker continued. "He wants you to come into Phillip sometime to give a statement about what hap-pened out there." He jerked his head toward the south. "They arrested Watson when he tried to get old Doc Swanson to dig a small bullet out of his shoulder. Claimed he didn't know what happened. He was just out on the Bad River Road and got out of his truck to haul an antelope carcass off the road when the bullet came from nowhere. Didn't even hear the shot. He drove on into Phillip to the doc's place. The sheriff sent a man out to check on his story and they found an an-telope carcass where he said it was."

"That ain't true!" I blurted.

"I know. But you gotta look at it from the sheriff's viewpoint. At any rate, he's gonna hold Watson for a day or two until we can get you in there to talk with the sheriff."

He moved out of the way as I rose and walked shakily to the desk. I ignored the spoon on the tray and picked up the bowl of soup in both hands and sipped, then drank it down, sucking the noodles out of the bowl. I walked over to the bureau and pulled out clean clothes and headed down toward the bathroom.

"I'm gonna get cleaned up and call Pa in Pierre and see how Mom's doing. You go down and saddle our horses so we can check on the stock. I think you might be right about that storm, and we gotta be ready to ride the stock."

"You need to get in to the sheriff—" he began, but I interrupted.

"The sheriff can wait. We got stock to tend and Pa's gone."

"I dunno," he said, shaking his head doubtfully.

"If it ain't snowing by noon, I'll head on into Pierre to see Mom."

"But the sheriff—"

"The sheriff ain't family," I said softly. "I'll call Johnny Stone and maybe his father will let him come over and give you a hand stock sitting until I can get back. I'll take the pickup."

"You ain't old enough to drive," he said. "And there's the sheriff—"

"I've been driving that pickup around the ranch for a year now. I reckon I can drive it on into Pierre. Now you best be going and saddling our horses. I'll be down soon as I get cleaned up."

He stared long and hard at me for a minute, his jaw working like he was fixing to argue with me. But I reckon he could tell that I was in no mood to be contradicted, and he turned and soundlessly gathered the tray from the desk and clumped down the hall to the stairs. I turned and entered the bathroom.

Noon came and so did the snow and we worked the cattle hard during the blow. Stocker's face was grim, and I knew he was thinking that what I was doing was all wrong, but I could also see a grudging respect behind his eyes and in the set of his face. The blizzard took the telephone lines, so we were pretty cut off from everything other than what went on in our own tiny world with the home pasture and ranch yard. In the afternoon of the second day, I had Stocker take an ax and chop the ice away from the stock tank so the cattle could drink. While he was doing that, I hooked up the Harvester tractor to a flatbed and brought bales of hay down to the cattle so they could eat. One thing about cattle is they will always eat even when the wind's howling around their ears and the snow is blowing so you can't see ten feet in front of you.

On the third day the blizzard lifted, but the telephone lines were still out. I decided that I was going to try to make it into town in the pickup, but I only got a half-mile down the road before I slid off into the ditch and had to walk back and get Stocker to help me pull the pickup out with the tractor and bring it back to the ranch.

I went up to the attic and found Pa's old duffel bag and filled it with some clothes and tossed in Zane Grey's *Nevada* and *The Drift Fence* and had Stocker drive me on the tractor into Midland. There I found a trucker heading on into Pierre and hitched a ride with him after I called the sheriff and listened to him rant about me not coming into Phillip so he could hang on to Tubby Watson a little longer. But I hadn't and after forty-eight hours he'd had to cut Tubby loose. I told the sheriff to never mind about that, and he started sputtering about youngsters and their high-handed ways and dammit I'd better—and that was when I hung up the telephone and caught the ride with the trucker.

The maintainer and road crews had gone down Route 14 a little ahead of us, and we had little trouble until we got to Hayes, where a couple of cars had crashed head-on into each other and managed to block the highway for the better part of four hours until a couple of ranchers came by with their tractors and pulled the wrecks onto one lane of the two-lane highway. The trucker and I listened to Brace Beemer's *The Lone Ranger* on his radio while they loaded the bodies of the drivers and their injured passengers into the beds of two pickups, tied a tarp over them, and headed on into Pierre ahead of us.

It was late—almost ten that night—when we got into Pierre, and the trucker decided to take me on down Dakota Avenue to St. Mary's Hospital instead of dropping me off at the bus station like he was planning on doing before we got slowed by the car wreck. I made real sure I thanked him greatly before I got out in front of the hospital and he drove away.

I found Pa in the waiting room just inside the front door across from the desk and switchboard. His face looked gray and tired, his eyes red-rimmed, black stubble covering his jaw. His black-and-white-checked flannel shirt looked rumpled but was still neatly buttoned, and his jeans bagged at the knees from sitting so long. A look of relief swept over his face as he rose and came toward me. He took the duffel bag from me and gave me a hard hug.

"You worried the hell out of me, Samantha," he said.

"Sorry, Pa," I answered. I noticed he had called me "Samantha" and suddenly realized that we were probably coming to a turning point in our relationship. "It just seemed like something that needed doing."

He smiled, then said, "How's the stock?"

"Fine, Pa," I answered. I could wait no longer. "How's Mom?" I asked.

He shook his head. "It don't look good," he said roughly. He looked away, but not before I saw tears welling in his eyes. He pulled a bandanna from his back pocket and blew his nose.

"They're operating now, trying to cut out the cancer."

I wanted to ask him why the two of them hadn't told me about this before, but I held my tongue and nodded silently. If Pa and Mom had wanted me to know, then they would have told me. Otherwise, it was understood that what was happening was between them and no one else. It went without saying that I wouldn't tell others about it, and Pa had told Stocker only enough for him to be able to tell me when he found me. And I knew Stocker wouldn't tell anyone, either. He had worked for Pa long enough to know that one didn't carry another's business to the bar or steak house. You don't talk about another man's cattle or his land, or ask about them, which was worse.

And so we waited, and I told Pa what had happened over the past few days. I told him about the ride I had made with the Christmas gifts for the Six Feathers family, being shot at, Tubby Watson showing up in Phillip with a .22 bullet in him, and how I hadn't called the sheriff because I was too busy with the stock. His eyes lit up at this and he nodded slowly, clumsily patting my shoulder.

"We take care of our own business," he said roughly. "You did good, Sam. Real good. Don't worry about Tubby. I think everything will be all right on that score."

"A shame about Rose Marie's doll," I said. "I'll get her another."

A tiny smile flickered at the corners of his lips. "That would be nice. I'm certain that she will like it. Even if Christmas is gonna have to be a bit late this year."

"They coming in?"

He nodded. "As soon as the weather clears. That storm blew up across the Badlands and locked down the road coming from Rapid City. They got as far as New Underwood before the road closed down in front of them. They tried to go back, but they were forced to stay there. Fred Welsh put them up."

"Grandma and Grandpa?" I asked.

"They're with Flo and Jimmy," he said. "Grandpa went out to take care of the cabin at Hill City and dropped Grandma off to visit some with Flo."

"Uh-huh," I said. I tried to smile. "Ain't been much of a Christmas, has it?"

He shook his head sadly. "Nope. Sure ain't."

The door to the waiting room opened, and a doctor wearing a surgical gown with a mask dangling from his neck came in. He paused, rubbed his hand tiredly over his face, and looked at Pa and me sitting in the corner. He had a greasy forehead and a large blackhead on the end of his nose. He came toward us, shoulders bowed as if carrying a bale of hay across them. We rose to meet him. He paused and looked at Pa, and I felt my stomach lurch before he even spoke.

"I'm sorry, Mr. McCaslin," he said quietly. His hands wove spirals in the air as he talked. "We did our best, but we couldn't get it all."

"How is she?" Pa asked quietly. I could hear the steel in his voice and knew he was holding everything in.

"Resting quietly enough," the doctor said. "When she's better, we'll send her to Rochester for chemotherapy and radiation. Right now, we've done all that we can do for her here."

"We'll let you know," Pa said. "Can we see her?"

The doctor glanced at me, frowned, and shook his head. "I need—"

"No, not now," Pa said. "We need to talk first. Then we'll let you know. Now, can we see her?"

"I understand," the doctor said quietly. "I'll send a nurse in to get you when she wakes up."

"I'm obliged," Pa said. "And thank you for what you've done."

The doctor started to say something again about Rochester, but a quick look at the set to Pa's face stopped him. He nodded and left, and Pa and I sat back down and waited. There wasn't much else to do except that, and I knew at the time that the waiting had only begun and a great sadness filled me like a huge ache.

The nurse came for us about two hours later. I excused myself after asking where the room was, telling Pa that I had to go to the bathroom first. I picked up the duffel bag and went into the bathroom and took out the blue gingham dress with the little lace collar that Grandma had given me for my birthday. It took me a minute or two to figure out how to button it up the back, but I did. My eyes were gritty and I washed my face the best I could in the sink. Then I took the duffel bag and made my way down the pale green corridor to Mom's room. She was groggy, but her eyes and lips smiled at me when I walked through the door. It took her a moment to register that I was wearing a dress, then tears sparkled in her eyes. I glanced at Pa. His mouth hung open, and when he saw me staring at him, he shut it and took his bandanna out of his back pocket and busied himself blowing his nose.

"So, you're home," she said weakly. Pa moved to the far side of the bed and sat, taking her hand clumsily in his own. She gave him a tired smile, then looked back at me. "You look nice, Samantha. Real nice."

"Like a little lady," Pa said huskily.

"Yeah, well, I reckon all things gotta change sometime or the other," I said, embarrassed.

"Where've you been? You had us really worried there."

I told her about how I had been stewing all night about what kind of Christmas the Six Feathers family was going to have and how I decided that they needed the Christmas more than we did, given all that they had been through over the past month. So I had gathered the presents, saddled my horse, and rode down to their place with them. I held back from telling her about Tubby Watson and glanced up at Pa. He gave a slight nod of his head, knowing that I had deliberately held back to keep her from worrying and stewing. She had enough on her table at the moment. There would be time for that later. She smiled and squeezed my hand.

"I'm proud of you," she said softly. "This has been a good Christmas." She reached out and gently touched my dress, and tears sparkled again in her eyes. "You look real nice, Samantha."

For a moment I was confused, wondering if she really understood how I had wrecked Christmas for all of us. She sensed my confusion and shook her head.

"Christmas isn't the presents, Sam," she said patiently. "It's what the presents mean."

"Yeah, I know. The three kings," I said.

"No," she said. "It means someone cares for another person enough to want to make them happy. To remind them that they aren't alone in the world. You see, everyone is his brother's keeper. I think you know that, now, and knowing that you know that makes this a wonderful Christmas for me."

Then I realized what she had meant about the meaning of Christmas, and I felt my youth slip away from me as we stood together, a family, in her hospital room.

Chapter XII

We managed to get through to Stocker the next day and told him that we would have Johnny Stone come over to help him with the stock until we could get home. Pa and I made a quick trip home to get clothes two days later and to check on the stock, then went right back to Pierre and the hospital. We told Mom what the doctor had said and she took it quietly for a long while, then said that she figured she had had enough of doctors and hospitals for a while and maybe she would feel differently about it all later, but right now she just wanted to go home. The doctor fought us about that, but Pa took him aside and spoke quietly to him.

We thought Mom would be coming home for New Year's, but she had a relapse and, for a while, we thought we'd lost her. But Mom slowly recovered, and at the end of January she came home. I was back in school and had put all thoughts of Tubby Watson out of my mind. Mrs. Six Feathers came over quite often to help out in the house, and Sarah and her brother came along, too. Her brother tagged along behind me, so I had to learn fast not to turn too quickly for fear of running over him. I really didn't have much to fear from that, for he kept up a running barrage of questions that left me pretty exhausted during the day and I took gratefully to saddling up and riding the draws and gullies around our land. A couple of times I saw men on horseback up in the hills and thought about riding over to check on them, as they seemed to be watching the ranch. But something always seemed to draw my attention away from that, and I forgot about them until it was too late to do anything.

Spring came early that year and the snow was pretty well gone except in the deep gullies where it lay like a dirty bank protected from the sun. Good Friday was warm, almost hot, that April, and the plum trees and pin cherries were budding out. I decided to take a ride over to the old homestead and see if I could find some Dutchman's-breeches flowering to bring back for Mom. Sometimes, when we had warm weather early, they would bring out their little white flowers that look like inverted sacks. I might even find some early-blooming bloodroot, and that would make a swell bouquet of wildflowers to surprise her with.

So I saddled Spotty and headed over. The sun felt good on my shoulders as I rode, even bringing a little sweat out to trickle down my back. I felt lazy and let Spotty pick his own way, nudging him gently with my heels to keep him moving when he paused to snatch a mouthful of grama grass from the fresh tufts scattered over the prairie. About halfway there, I saw a couple of riders moving along the south hill line. I thought they had rifles sticking up in the air and wondered idly if they were hunting coyotes. I watched as they dipped down along a ridgeline and disappeared in a coulee. I kept waiting to see if they came up the other side, but they didn't. I came to the end of the pasture and had let myself out through the gate to follow Bad River on down to the homestead when I heard a single gunshot in the distance. I paused and looked around, but I didn't see anything. I mounted and rode on down the next couple of miles to where the railroad trestle cut over the small gully and dismounted, tying Spotty on a long lead to one of the creosote timbers.

I made my way through the chokecherry bushes to the old house and found him lying next to the rusted pump, facedown, his arms sprawled out in front of him, his fingers hooked deep into the thick grass. The toes of his boots had dug a deep furrow in the ground; he'd died hard. I didn't have to roll him over to know it was Tubby Watson, but I did anyway. A single bullet had hit him up high in the belly just below his breastbone. A small trickle of blood curled from one corner of his mouth, his lips drawn back in a frozen rictus of pain. His eyes were half-closed.

I backed away carefully, looking around half-fearfully, wondering if whoever had shot him was still lurking around, but I didn't see anyone until I made it back out through the chokecherry bushes to my horse. I mounted and turned Spotty to ride back to the ranch, and then I saw them sitting quietly on their horses, rifles balanced across the pommels of their saddles, watching me from a small hill above the trestle. Two Indians, motionless, their faces expressionless. I didn't know them, yet for some reason I raised my hand and waved. One of them waved back; then they turned their horses and rode south toward the river, heading back toward the reservation.

Relieved, I turned my horse's nose and rode briskly back to the ranch. I found Pa puttering around in the barn and told him what I had found and said I would ride up to the house and telephone the sheriff. He stopped me and stared reflectively up at the house, then shook his head.

"No sense worrying your mother any," he said. "You call

the sheriff and let him know that Tubby Watson had come back around and you'll have to tell her the whole story. The preacher's up there, too, and that would spread everything over the county. Never seen a person talk so much about things that ain't his concern. So far, it's died down without her hearing about it. Let's keep it that way."

"But there's Stocker—" I began.

"And he's in Pierre. I gave him the weekend off, remember?" Pa said. "I think it best if we handle this ourselves."

And so Pa saddled Fritz while I gathered a couple of spades, and together we rode back to the homestead. We buried him down in the old root cellar behind the old house. Pa had to kill a couple of rattlesnakes first and then allowed that he was certain that there were others in there and, if not, there would be before long and that would keep most people out. I knew he was talking about brush hunters during the grouse season, who liked to walk the railroad tracks and hunt the brush and tree lines in the fall.

We dug the grave down about three feet and wrapped him in an old painter's tarp that Pa had tied behind his saddle and we dropped Tubby Watson in and packed the dirt around him. It still looked suspiciously like a grave to me, but Pa said that it would settle in time.

We rode back home, pausing to pick a huge bouquet of early-blooming prairie flowers for Mom. She was tickled and laughed delightedly as we brought in the four vases brimming with the flowers to put around the living room where she lay on the sofa, a blanket tucked around her, reading W. Somerset Maugham's *The Razor's Edge*. She had been reading constantly since we brought her back home from the hospital. We had kept from mentioning Rochester again and I knew that the decision had been silently reached that there would be no chemotherapy, no radiation. Her cheeks had a rosy blush around them and she clapped her hands and demanded that Pa come over for a kiss, and then she gave me a hug and I remember the faint hint of lavender she wore and the ticking of the clock on the mantelpiece and the way the sun slatted in through the windows with the dust motes dancing in its beams. I remember thinking how brave she was, and I had to choke back a lump in my throat because I didn't want her to see me cry. I realized then that bravery was something that had to be re-created daily with quiet dignity and that the daily trials she put up with silently were a moral victory.

That was the last bouquet we brought to her. She died two days later, quietly in her sleep, while Pa and I were working with the spring calves down at the corral. At first we thought she was asleep when we came back in the house to check on her. Her eyes were closed and she had a small smile upon her lips. Her skin was so fine that you could read the Bible through it.

I wore that blue gingham dress to her funeral and drew quite a few stares when Pa and me walked into the church together. Rose Marie gave me a hard look, then pretended not to notice. But the boys did, and I knew things had changed since my ride. That night in the old house, waiting for Watson to come around and do to me what he had done to Sarah, had made me rethink things a bit. I still felt awkward in the dress, but the way Johnny Stone took to looking at me—well, it made me feel kind of funny and fuzzy inside.

It was a real nice service, and the reverend didn't ramble on so much that Pa got restless. But I got the strange feeling that Pa probably wouldn't have gotten restless anyway on this particular day. It wasn't just Mom's funeral; it was something else, too. It was learning who I was.

We buried Mom up by the big cottonwood tree on a hill over the tank in the home pasture, and I rode down to the old homestead and dug up some prairie violets and a small meadow rose to plant on her grave. Pa built a white picket fence around her grave to keep the cattle away. I noticed he left room for a couple of other graves as well, but I didn't say anything about that and he didn't volunteer his reasoning. I guess he really didn't have to. It was a family matter and we took care of our own.